I Wanna Love You

Tina J

Copyright 2017

This novel is a work of fiction. Any resemblances to actual events, real people, living or dead, organizations, establishments or locales are products of the author's imagination. Other names, characters, places, and incidents are used fictionally.

More Books by Tina J

A Thin Line Between Me & My Thug 1-2
I Got Luv for My Shawty 1-2
Kharis and Caleb: A Different kind of Love 1-2
Loving You is a Battle 1-3
Violet and the Connect 1-3
You Complete Me
Love Will Lead You Back
This Thing Called Love
Are We in This Together 1-3
Shawty Down to Ride For a Boss 1-3
When a Boss Falls in Love 1-3
Let Me Be The One 1-2
We Got That Forever Love
Ain't No Savage Like The One I got 1-2
A Queen & Hustla 1-2 (collab)
Thirsty for a Bad Boy 1-2
Hasaan and Serena: An Unforgettable Love 1-2
We Both End Up With Scars
Are We in this Together 1-3
Caught up Luvin a beast 1-3
A Street King & his Shawty 1-2
I Fell for the Wrong Bad Boy 1-2 (collab)
Addicted to Loving a Boss 1-3
I need that Gangsta Love 1-2 (collab)
Still Luvin' a Beast 1-2
I Wanna Love You 1-2
When She's Bad, I'm Badder 1-3

Honor

Hello everyone. My name is Honor Chestnut and I'm a victim of circumstance. I know some of you may laugh and hell, I laugh too but let me explain what I mean.

Honor Chestnut, who is myself, grew up in the hood. I'm not talking just in some apartments that mainly black folk lived in. I'm talking the straight gutta. Roaches, mice, urine in the hallways, broken elevators, murders in broad daylights, car jacking's, rapes and the list could go on and on, but you know where I'm going with it. We had housing assistance and my moms' rent was only fifty dollars and her food stamps were a little over four hundred. We stretched that shit to the end of the month every time and if we ran out, well lets just say we didn't.

My mom was a straight alcoholic, slash junkie who did anything and everyone to get a hit; even some of the teenage boys I went to school with. However, she has never, ever, once tried to sell me, put me on the corner or even had me looking like a piece of shit. She stole from stores to make sure I had what I needed. It may not have been expensive items but Honor Chestnut did not, and I repeat, did not walk around in ripped up clothes unless they were made that way, high waters, busted open sneakers or anything that would make me look a mess.

Now back to the reason why I'm the victim of circumstance. I feel this way because as a high school and college graduate, I'm still in the ghetto. I have my own spot and it's not in the suburbs but around the corner from where I grew up. I haven't found me a dope boy or kingpin like some of these chicks to move me out of here. Shit, they were all taken and the corner boys were just that, boys. There was one guy I used to be with. He was older than me by four years and the love of my life.

Abe Saunder was the epitome of fine to me at the tender age of sixteen. He was light skin with gray eyes, I know it sounds weird but it wasn't. He had the beard thing going on and he kept his hair in a low cut fade. He had tattoos all over and would tell me all the time he wasn't finished. His body was on the skinny side but I knew it wouldn't last long because he was always in the gym. And he only had eyes for me, or so I thought.

In the beginning he could do no wrong, however, there was this chick named Vera who lived next door to him and she hated me. I'm not sure why, when he was my man. Everyone knew we were together but often when we did go out, I'd get stares from chicks and during some nights, I'd get anonymous calls from someone and it sounded like they were having sex. I can admit, sometimes I would listen but the woman's voice would get annoying as hell and I'd have to hang up. I mean she'd be screaming like someone was killing her, instead of fucking her.

Come to find out later, it was my so-called boyfriend Abe making her scream. I only found out because one day, Vera and her friends stood outside the stoop at my building and couldn't wait to discuss it. I refused to cry because my momma taught me, "*If someone knows they upset you enough to make you cry, they'll keep coming for you. Suck it up and cry later.*" It's exactly what I did.

They followed me walking down the street and Vera

told me she fucked him til the early morning. None of it bothered me but when she said the words, "*I'm pregnant, so leave him alone.*" My feet stopped moving for a second. I felt the tears coming and tried my best to stop them. It was no use, and I ran as fast as my sixteen-year-old feet could take me. I made it to Abe's house and he was just pulling up.

I confronted him and he took me in the house and explained some dumb ass story about how she couldn't let go. Unfortunately for him, she showed up with the ultrasound and proof of them indeed being together. She showed me pictures, videos, text messages and if that weren't enough, she lifted his shirt and showed the two hickeys she left on his chest the previous night. Again, I went running away and didn't stop until I got to the corner store.

I called my best friend Roxanne and asked her to meet me. As I waited, my greedy ass brought a soda, some chips and candy. I eat a lot of sweets when I get upset. Two guys from the block were coming down the street and both of them hated me. They were disrespectful as hell and would grab my ass or call me bitches because I was one of the last virgins alive, as they say.

Anyway, I should've taken my ass in the store but I stood there ignoring them as usual. I felt someone jerk my arm and all my stuff fell. My mouth was covered and the gun in my side kept me from trying to fight. I was pulled into an alley and thrown on the ground. I looked to see who it was and the two guys who hated me were now smiling down.

I began kicking and screaming until the gun cocked. I was brutally raped and beaten by both of them. I'm not even sure when I was found. All I know is, I woke up in the hospital with my mom, best friend and an angry Abe and Noah. The two of them were cousins and tight like glue.

I couldn't even lie and tell them I didn't know who did it because evidently, someone saw them run out the alley. The person figured something wasn't right if they came out of there because it's a spot where murders have allegedly been committed. Abe and Noah let me know the situation was handled without telling me the story.

Everyone stepped out to give us a minute and I refused to look at him. I didn't forget he cheated or that the chick was pregnant. He sat next to me on the bed and it was the first time I broke down. I cried for what happened to me, I cried for him getting her pregnant and I cried knowing, the love of my life is gone.

He tried to comfort me but I pushed him away and asked for him never to contact me again. The begging and apologizing started and I wanted to take him back, I just couldn't. The love I had, he took for granted. I was a virgin and no, I wasn't ready to have sex but it didn't mean he was supposed to go sleep with someone else. I guess it's what I get for being with an older guy.

A week after my rape, Abe was arrested and eventually given fifteen years for manslaughter with the possibility of parole in ten. I thought about writing him, however, I didn't want to become caught up in loving him again or getting in between what Vera claimed they had going on. Noah told me on plenty of occasions Abe wanted to see me or asked if he could write. I told Noah to tell him not to waste ink or lead on a piece of paper I'd never read.

So I say again, I am a victim of circumstance because I

fall into the rape statistic category, loser ass boyfriend, heart broken chick from the ghetto and last but not least BROKEN! But don't feel sad for me because I won't for the next bitch.

****

Over the years I've grown into a woman who knew her worth and set goals for myself, which didn't include a man. Yes, I yearned to be touched like women I saw on television or the ones I read about in books, but no one could get close enough to me after Abe. I constantly compared them and because of it, it never worked.

Here it is eleven years later and Abe is coming home. Noah went to pick him up today so Roxanne and I decided to do some shopping, where she dropped a ball on me by mentioning a welcome home party. I wasn't ready to see him nor did I want to be bothered with his petty ass baby mama, who had something to say each time she laid eyes on me. After begging me, I finally gave in.

"This is going to be so much fun. Yea." I said in a childish like voice and rolled my eyes.

"Don't be like that Honor. You have your life and he's coming home to restart his. If you don't want to speak, then don't but lets have fun. Shit, we deserve it." I nodded my head but knew I would regret saying yes.

Abe

Damn it felt good to be home. After being locked down for eleven years, I appreciated the smallest shit, like taking a shower in peace, and eating when I felt like it. The most important thing I appreciated, was being here for my daughter. Even though I've been a part of her life since she was born, it was from jail, but she knew who I was. One thing no one could take from me was my relationship with her. Vera may get on my nerves but she always made sure to keep her in my life and I will always love her for that.

Chelsea was my heart and she was a daddy's girl to the fullest. She is ten years old, smart as hell and beautiful. She wrote me a letter every week about how school is, who she did or didn't like and told me the trifling shit her mom did. I would tell her not to mention it, because it would piss me off but she couldn't help it.

I never told her mom about any of the stuff Chelsea wrote to me but I got in Vera's ass one day she bought my daughter here, about her having sex in the house. I'm not the type of nigga to have a female waiting, knowing I'm doing a bid this long, but the least you could have done was sex these niggas elsewhere. My daughter told me how her mom makes weird noises and the guy used to come out in only boxers. That alone, had my blood boiling. The day I confronted Vera the officers threw me in a hole for a week because I tried to snap her damn neck.

A man walking out in his boxers at a woman's house with the knowledge of her having a daughter is suspect as hell to me. He didn't know if Chelsea would come out and what if his ass is a pedophile? Some women think because their dude is known on the streets or he loves her, they won't even attempt to look at a child but that's far from the truth. I don't know how many men I've run across in the jail whose here for that very same reason.

The woman trusted him around her kid, the temptation came and he took their innocence. It happens all the time but it won't to my daughter. I bet she didn't have any more men at the house and if she did, my daughter didn't witness or hear anything about it.

Vera's trifling ass couldn't wait to drop her off to me when I got home; talking about its my time to raise her. That was last week and I haven't seen or heard from her since, but I wasn't surprised at all. Hell the bitch shitted on me when I was locked up. She didn't keep money on my books; the only time she visited was to bring my child. And her ass was living in the house I brought and driving the brand new car I purchased before I got knocked. Again, she didn't have to stop her life but damn if it weren't for my mom or my cousin Noah, a nigga would've been stuck like a motherfucker in here.

Every time I thought about Vera fucking me over I reminisce about Honor. She was the love of my life and I fucked up for some pussy. Honor, had gone through some shit in her life and wasn't ready to open herself all the way. She wasn't comfortable with the way her moms' lifestyle was and told me she wasn't ready to give her innocence to anyone yet. I respected her decision to make me wait because we all know; virginity isn't something a woman can get back.

I cheated a few times but only sexually. What I mean by that is, these women didn't get my money, attention or anything else for that matter. My time with them was spent on fucking and that's it. Honor was and is still the only woman who could get anything she wanted from me, no questions asked. I owed her that for hurting her the way I did. I was young and dumb but I wouldn't change shit I did because my daughter wouldn't be here and that would be saying I regret her. I just hate that Honor was the one who got away.

Tonight was my welcome home party and I really wasn't feeling the shit but Noah wouldn't give up. Plus, I had a feeling I'd get to see Honor's fine ass. I knew what the hell her little ass had been up to because I kept up with her through Roxanne and Noah. She had a good ass job and still lived in the hood. I guess she finally made it out the projects; however, she was still there on a regular because her mom refused to move. Roxanne said she offered to move her mom hundreds of times, but her mom said she'd die before leaving.

She spent some nights with her mom as well and Noah told me he had people watching her at all times. Even though

15

she had no idea, he did it for me. I couldn't protect Honor the way I wanted in here and I blame myself for what happened to her. Had I not cheated, she would have never run away from me and into the arms of those idiots. No one and I mean no one will ever hurt her again if I can help it. She didn't know but I was snatching her ass up and planned on finally putting a ring on her finger. She belonged to me, always have and always will.

My daughter was already at my moms for the night so I was free to party late and I planned on getting fucked up. It had been too long since I hung with my people and I was going to enjoy it to the fullest. Yeah the king was home and it was time to let mothafuckas know and get back to business. As far as running these streets, I'm not sure its what I want though. Eleven years is a long damn time and to even think about going back made my stomach hurt.

Noah was my cousin and we were close as hell, shit, he was the only nigga I trusted and he's proven his loyalty time and time again. I went away eleven years ago with a nice amount of money saved and came home two weeks ago to over

6 million. He invested in stocks, a barbershop and a few apartment buildings that were doing pretty well. Never once did he complain about what he did for me or mention how I should pay him back. I owed him everything.

Shit, it's because of him my daughter ate while I was away. Even though Vera didn't

deserve shit, he made sure her and my daughter kept a roof over their heads and bills were paid. People think because you're family, they have to help you, but family doesn't make anyone do anything. When you're at your lowest moment, you will see who's down for you. Yeah, that nigga was loyal without a doubt, and I'll forever be grateful for that shit.

****

I was chilling at home, smoking a blunt and amping myself up for this party. Noah and I went shopping earlier today and the clothes I chose were simple. It was an all black Versace outfit with the black leather high top sneakers to match. Noah gave me a diamond-encrusted necklace with a cross on it as a welcome home gift and my mom and Chelsea got me some diamond studs. Yea, Chelsea said she brought them but its all good. The Rolex I picked up a few days ago accentuated the outfit well and the fresh haircut and shave topped it off. Say what you want but a nigga was fresh to death and planned on getting in some pussy.

Years of getting pussy behind prison walls from the correction officers in closets and other small areas is nothing compared to getting it out in the open, without worrying someone will catch you. I grabbed my money, keys, and anything else I needed, jumped in my range and headed to pick Noah up. Tonight is going to be epic and a nigga couldn't wait.

"What up cuz? You ready to be welcomed back." Noah asked closing the door and passing me the blunt.

"Hell yea. I hope you set up some strippers or something." He put his head down laughing.

"You know I got you. Don't be trying to get me in trouble with my girl by getting carried away. We are on good terms right now and I want to keep it that way."

"You may as well marry her ass. Shit, y'all been together for a long time, got two kids and she is your down ass chick. I know that and so does every bitch on the streets." We both laughed.

Roxanne and Noah have been together for a long time but not the way people think. We've known her for years but she wouldn't give Noah the time of day. She always told him to find her when he was ready to settle down. He did eventually lock her down and they've been rocking ever since but not without the problems most couples go through.

"I have the ring my nigga. I had to wait for your incarcerated ass to be released to propose."

"What were you waiting on me for?"

"Because her ass is going to want to marry me right away and my best man had to be there."

"Oh shit nigga. You trying to make me cry?" I let my index finger fall down my eye in a dramatic form.

"Fuck you nigga. I'll be sure to pick someone off the street to stand next to me, while you're sitting on the pew with everyone else."

"Yea fucking right. If I ain't up there, no one else will be either. Fuck you think this is."

"You better act like you appreciate me choosing your ass. Shit, Roxanne claim she just wants me and her at the altar whenever we do it."

"Wait! She knows?"

"Hell no. She be leaving subliminal messages on my texts about how it would feel to be a married woman, or she'll pick up a wedding magazine and make me look at a dress while standing in line at the grocery store. You know the slick shit women do to get your attention."

"What you say when she does it?"

"I be like, you better find that nigga the woman in the magazine buying the dress for and see if he'll marry your ass."

"You ain't shit."

"Nope. That's what her ass gets. I don't need her giving me hints. She knows neither of us are going anywhere and one day she'll be my wife. Her impatient ass has to wait. If I'm the one proposing it's on my time and when she picks the wedding date, it's on hers." I shook my head laughing at him. My cousin is shot the hell out.

We parked in the lot of the club and got out to see the line wrapped around the corner. To see all the love for me from the streets had me feeling good. I'm not going to lie and say I don't miss the street life but the time spent in jail, definitely makes me think twice before turning back to them.

Security gave us a pound and lifted the rope for us to go in. It was packed wall to wall and the women were bad. I've seen chicks on television who looked beautiful but seeing some up close is a different story. I wonder what they look like under all the makeup, spanx and other shit holding them together though.

"What can I get for you?" The waitress asked as we made our way to the area sectioned off for us. I would call it VIP but this club didn't have one so this would do.

"I'll take two shots of Henny." Noah put his order in and she stepped off.

All through the night dudes were coming up to speak as well as women. I received a ton of phone numbers and sexual favors promised if I took them home. The love was real and had it not been for Honor walking in, I may have taking a

21

couple of these women with me but once my eyes laid on her, she was the only thing on my mind and the only one I wanted to take home.

She was still gorgeous and her body was a tad bit smaller than what she used to be, but overall her beauty still captivated me. The dress she wore came to the top of her knee and the back was out, exposing the tattoo with my name on her shoulder. I smiled and took a sip of my drink. I thought she would have gotten in removed by now but I see she didn't. Hell, I had her name tatted on the top of my hand before getting locked up and got her name going across my back in jail.

Niggas swarmed her and Roxanne like prey in the jungle. I gave her space but planned on speaking when the time is right. Noah told me Roxanne said she didn't want to come but I'm grateful she did. After watching and allowing these women to entertain me, I made my approach.

"Hello Honor." I whispered in her ear after walking to where she was. Her body froze and when she turned around the waterworks started.

"Don't cry ma." She backed away and bumped into Roxanne.

"You ok Honor."

"Yea. I'm ready to go." Roxanne gave me a dirty look.

"I didn't do anything so fix your face before I get Noah over here to do it for you." She rolled her eyes.

"Don't leave Honor." I reached out for her hand and when we touched it was as if the feelings we had came rushing back. I know she felt it too. Neither of us let the other one's hand go and we stood there staring at each another.

"It's nice to see you." She finally let go, picked up her things and headed for the door.

"Then why are you running away?" I grabbed her arm gently so she wouldn't assume I was being rough.

"Abe, I -" Was all she could get out before Vera came over.

"You still chasing this bitch?" Vera said.

"And you're still a stalker. You'll learn one day that pussy isn't what keeps a man; especially when another woman has his heart." I smirked.

"I may not have his heart here." She pointed to my chest.

"But I have his heart at home with her grandmother." Honor didn't say anything. Vera can say all the shit she wants but it's never been a secret about how I felt when it came to Honor.

"Vera get the fuck out of here." I hate she threw in Honor's face about having my child.

"I'm tired of this bitch thinking she's better than me. Well, guess what bitch. I gave him his first-born. Something, you'll never, ever get. Say what you want but this man will always be in my life and his dick will too. You were slacking in your relationship boo, that's why he dipped out."

"This is why I didn't want to come here Roxanne. Can you take me home please?" She shoulder checked Vera who was laughing hard as hell with her friends.

"Honor, wait!" I tried to get her attention but it was so many people trying to get mine, I lost her in the crowd.

Damn!

"Honor you can't let her get you upset every time you see her. She knows how to get under your skin and you let her." I told her walking to the car.

"I know but it's hard because she's right about all of it. He did dip out, have a child with her and will always be in her life. I can't compare to that."

"Abe doesn't care about Vera. Do you know how many times Noah told me he hated her. She did a lot of grimy shit while he was in jail and he won't forgive her. Don't forget you were always the main chick. She's mad he won't allow her that spot, ever. Abe has it reserved for his boo and that is you." I pointed as she drove me home.

"Did you see how fine he was? Girl, if I had sex with men, I would've been all over it."

"You not having sex is something you're holding on too." She looked at me crazy.

"I'm not saying what you went through isn't traumatic but honey it's holding you back from experiencing a lot. It's been years Honor and is time you allowed yourself to be loved.

25

That man loves you and if you don't want him fine, but don't get mad when you see other women around him either." She nodded her head.

"And what were you about to cry for when he approached you?"

"Girl, I don't know. My emotions were all over the place when I laid eyes on him."

"Umm hmmm. That's because you need some dick in your life, real or fake."

"Fake."

"Hell yea bitch! Don't think lesbian women who've had men before don't miss the dick. Instead of cheating or if they're alone you can guarantee they using one. Hell, I'm not one and the nights Noah pisses me off, I damn sure fuck myself."

"Really!"

"Hell yea. I'll have the bullet on my clit and my toy inside. It may not be the real thing but it's definitely satisfying and I can cum a lot. If you ask me, Lesbian women winning."
We both busted out laughing.

She parked in front of my house and I stepped out after

giving her a hug. We said our goodbyes and she waited for me to open the door before pulling off. The house was quiet so I made sure to take my heels off because they echoed loud as hell on these hardwood floors.

I went up the steps and checked in on my daughter Precious who was seven and my son, Noah Junior who was nine. He only answered if you called him Junior and only his father could call him by his real name and he'd answer. That kid is a piece of work but the only person he didn't fuck with, is Noah.

Precious was laid out on her bed with the television blasting as always. I keep telling her she's going to go deaf. I peeked in Junior's room and he too was knocked the hell out. His television was on but the volume was down and his laptop was on his bed. I closed the door and went to take a shower to get the sweat off my body.

It was hot as hell in the club, and between the dancing Honor and I did and all the thirsty niggas, a bitch felt dirty. After I got out, I checked my phone and noticed a voicemail from Noah. He didn't usually leave one but maybe it was important. I hit the icon to retrieve it and put it on speaker as I rubbed lotion on my legs. My face frowned up as I listened to the message.

I picked my phone up, tracked his, and left out the house. His mom still had her door open so if the kids woke up she would hear them. She stayed with us on the weekends in case we decided to go out. She always told us we were young and should enjoy ourselves. As of lately, she's been real shady and I don't know why. I planned on speaking to Noah about it tomorrow but here I am off to fuck shit up.

I parked in front of the address the GPS led me to and had to close my mouth. The house was huge and there were people everywhere. Half naked women and niggas smoking and drinking, scattered the lawn. I stepped in the house and it was the same shit going on. I didn't see Noah but Abe had two women on his lap.

I didn't let him see me because he would definitely warn Noah. I walked around the house and opened every close door I saw downstairs. Some man approached me and asked for my number. He was fine as hell and had I not been in a relationship and here to kill my man, I may have given it to him.

"Hey do you know Noah? He told me to meet him here." I said in a sultry voice.

"Damn, that nigga gets all the women." He looked me up and down licking his lips.

"Oh you have these parties all the time?" I questioned him without letting him know my real reason for being here.

"Yea. I've had these now for about a year and a half. I only have them every other month though. He usually drinks, smokes and leaves but tonight some chicks offered him to go upstairs and he went." I nodded my head.

"Wow. That's great I guess. Where did you say Noah was?"

"Oh. He's up in the room with the blue sign on it."

"Blue sign?" I raised my eyebrow.

"Yea. Each room has a sign on it and whatever it says the women have to do."

I laughed and made my way up there. I passed a room with a sign that said Anal on it. (*He loves when we do this*) I opened the door and he wasn't in there. The next door said

Fisting. (*White people shit*) I didn't even bother opening that or

the Gay one. This one said Orgy. (*I can see his nasty ass in

here*) but he wasn't in here either.

There were a few more doors that led down the hall

and sure enough they all had different color signs. It felt as if I

were walking in a porn sight with all these rooms. I checked

them all and came upon the last one. Seeing he wasn't in any

of those, he had to be in here. I stopped and looked up at the

door and it surely had a blue sign on it. "*Anything Goes*" Hmph.

I hated to see what the sign meant but here I am

opening it. I couldn't believe my eyes. Noah was hitting some

bitch from the back, well she was throwing her ass because he

didn't seem to be moving. Another one allowed a chick to fuck

her pussy with a damn beer bottle. The chick he was screwing,

was eating out a woman laid on the bed. While another chick

sat on top of her face.

"If you ask me, this should be the orgy room. I mean

more than two usually means that." Noah turned around slowly and pulled his dick out of the woman. I almost gagged when I saw he didn't have a condom on.

"Roxanne this isn't what it looks like." I tossed my head laughing and cocked my gun back. Yea, a bitch was holding and he knew I wasn't afraid to use it. The women began yelling and trying to grab their things up to leave.

"If you don't know by now Noah, its over."

"Baby, let me talk to you." His words were slurring and he could barely stand. It didn't affect him fucking this woman so I don't know why he's struggling now.

"There's nothing to talk about." He pulled his jeans up and attempted to come towards me.

BOOM! I let a shot off grazing his ear. I could hear people yelling outside the room.

"Roxanne, I'm sorrrrrrryyyyyy." His words were really fucked up. He started stumbling over the furniture.

BOOM! I let another shot off in his arm. He didn't budge as he stood there letting a few tears fall down his face.

"I swear I never meant to hurt you. I don't know what's going on or how I even got up here." He said and I now, felt

31

the tears coming down my face.

BOOM! I let one more off in his chest, turned around and walked out. I saw Abe standing at the bottom of the steps and when he looked in my hands, he took off upstairs. Talk all the shit you want but I've always told Noah if he cheated on me again, I'd kill him. I guess he thought a bitch was playing but he knows now, I'm not.

A few years ago, Noah cheated on me with some ghetto trash. I never told anyone because I was embarrassed and she lived in a different town. They were meeting up at a hotel a few times a month. I only found out because Honor peeped him when she was riding by and saw them going in. I told her she was his cousin from out of town. I'm not sure if she believed me but Honor never asked me about it afterwards.

Anyway, I sat outside the hotel waiting for him. He didn't exit until after one in the morning. She appeared to be happy and he had an attitude, which was weird. I jumped out the car and approached both of them. He couldn't say shit and she popped off at the mouth and of course, I beat her ass.

Come to find out he had gotten her pregnant and it was

too late to terminate it. I was so hurt, that after hearing it, I left him standing there and tried to run both of them over on my way out the parking lot, but missed. The baby is now three years old and it is his, because he took a paternity test.

The chick left the baby with her mom and hasn't looked back since. She didn't want the baby if she couldn't have Noah. I eventually took him back but I refused to accept the child. No, the baby has nothing to do with his infidelity, but seeing her reminds me of his cheating. I will give in one day and accept her but I can't right now.

"IF MY COUSIN DIES, I WILL FUCKING KILL YOU." Abe screamed in my ear as the EMT's placed Noah on a stretcher. The hate in his eyes was real and my heart was pounding when he said that. If he said something about killing you, you can bet he will do it. I should've left after shooting him but I had to know what happened.

"Does anyone know what happened here?" I turned around and saw a detective.

"No and we won't call you when we do. Beat it." Abe said and walked to his truck, speeding out behind the ambulance. I don't know why but I hopped in my car and went to the hospital. After sitting in the parking lot of the ER for an hour, I decided to go in. I assumed everyone wouldn't be there yet. I saw Abe, his mom and some other dudes. I didn't want them to see me and walked in a different direction. I heard Abe yell my name.

"You need to leave."

"Is he going to be ok?"

"Why do you care?"

"Abe you know how I feel about him."

"I knew how you felt."

"I'm sorry Abe. I told him if he ever cheated on me again I would kill him." I admitted with no regret.

"That nigga didn't cheat on you."

"Ugh, I walked in on him with his dick in another woman's pussy. I'm not sure what you consider cheating but in my eyes, that qualifies." He jacked me up by the shirt and tossed my ass against the wall.

"Somebody slipped something in his drink you dumb bitch. That nigga would never cheat on you again after what

34

happened before."

"How you know he was drugged?"

"The dude from the party called and told me he had a video of you shooting him. I asked him to send it to me and on it, there were angles from the house and some bitch slipped two things in his drink." I covered my mouth and broke down crying hard.

"Take that crying shit the fuck up out of here. Don't nobody want to hear it." He pushed me towards the door.

"I want to see him. Can I stay to make sure he's ok and apologize?"

"You'll know he's ok, if I don't show up to the house and murk your ass. Get the fuck out my face yo."

"Abe, please."

"Abe, what is going on? Why aren't you allowing her in?" His mom came up behind him asking.

"Roxanne has to get the kids so my aunt can come up here." He gave me this look telling me not to contest and I didn't."

"Ok. I'm going." I never woke Noah's mom up so she

had no idea he was shot and she never slept with her ringer on. I walked out the hospital and drove to my house thinking about how I may have killed my man.

****

SMACK!

"Bitch are you fucking crazy not telling me my son was shot." I grabbed my face and caught myself from hitting her.

"I wanted to check on him and give you good news. I didn't want you to worry. Who told you?" She snatched her keys up.

"His other baby mama." I grabbed her arm and she looked at me crazy.

"I don't give a fuck how you stare at me. This is my house and what you won't do is disrespect me. I'll give you that smack because I deserve it for not informing you but I would suggest you keep your hands to yourself and don't mention her in my house."

"You may scare those women on the streets but you pump no fear over here. Now you may get over because you're younger but honey, this old bitch is going to give you a run for

36

your money first."

"Yea ok." I opened the door for her to leave and she turned around.

"Do you know why he cheated on you in the first place?" I stood there with my arms folded. I had no idea why she even felt the need to bring his infidelity up.

"He was looking for someone to replace the bitch who aborted two of his kids, she thought he knew nothing about." I covered my mouth. I didn't speak of those abortions to anyone, not even Honor and she's my best friend.

"Exactly. My son finds out everything. However, he forgave you, because you forgave him for having a baby on you. I wish you didn't and he found a good woman who didn't stress him when he left the house."

"I didn't know you felt this way about me." she tossed her head and stared at me.

"I will play the part for my son but know this." She moved in closer.

"I don't like you and I'm going to make sure he knows you never told his mother. I had to be awakened out my sleep by some chick in his past about it. I wish it were you who was shot and died before the EMT's got there."

"Damn, if you feel that way, make sure you find somewhere to stay. Your ass is no longer welcomed here."

"Grandma, why did you say that to my mom? You want her dead?" My son asked coming down the steps. I had no idea he heard us but I guess the shouting woke him up.

"Junior."

"Get out grandma and don't come back." He told her.

"Who are you talking to little boy? I'll whoop yo ass."

"You ain't doing shit to my son. Keep testing me old lady."

"My dad told me when he's not around to protect my mom and sister. You want my mom dead and I know he's going to be mad you said it to her." He stood there with his arms folded looking just like Noah and I started crying. I tried hard to hold in the tears as she verbally attacked me but hearing my son protect me made me happy, but sad it had to be over his grandmother. He loved her but his mom comes first and he proved it.

"Keep these bad ass kids away from me. I'll make sure my other granddaughter, their sister Melody, takes their place." I punched her in the face and we went at it for a few minutes. I heard a gun go off and we both stopped. My son stood there pointing it at her.

"I don't know why you keep saying mean things to my mom but you have to go." He told her and she stood up fixing her clothes.

"You'll be hearing from me and my sister soon." Her and Abe's mom are in their early fifties but carried on like women in their twenties sometimes. If she said that it meant they were going to come jump me and I'm good. I'm not scared of them and hoped she came today since I'm in a fighting mood.

"I'll be waiting." Junior slammed the door in her face and came to where I just took a seat on the steps.

"Why did grandma say I had another sister?"

"Junior, can we talk about this when your dad comes home?"

"No ma. I want to know what she's talking about." I

39

hated that he was so smart and knew bullshit when he saw it. He was going to see straight through this story when I tell him.

"Umm. Almost four years ago daddy met someone and they had a baby. She is three years old and her name is Melody." He jumped up.

"Dad, cheated on you."

"Junior, calm down."

"Ma, did dad cheat on you?"

"He made a mistake Junior and I forgave him."

"Did you ma? If you did, why haven't we met her?"

"I'm not ready and I didn't want you being angry at daddy for his mistake."

"He made you weak." I heard my son mumble as he walked up the steps shaking his head. What the hell did he know about a woman being weak? Was I weak? This is exactly why I shielded them from the other woman. At twenty seven, I've dealt with a man who had a baby on me, his mom doesn't like me, shot the love of my life and had my son consider me to be weak. What else could go wrong?

"Ma, daddy cheated on you?" I heard Precious running

downstairs and looked up to see she had tears in her eyes. I hugged her and listened to her cry. I looked up to wipe my eyes and Junior stood there with hate in his eyes. Noah's mother just created a fucking monster.

Noah

I don't know what the hell happened to me. One minute, Abe and I go to my man Paul's house for one of his infamous parties and the next thing I remember, is my girl shooting me. The doctor's told me whatever went in my system was so strong, had I not been shot and brought in, most likely, I would've died.

I came out of a medically induced coma three days ago and I haven't seen my girl or my kids. However, Kasha and her mom brought my daughter up here and they were kicking it with my mom as if nothing went down. I wanted to find out what the hell was going on but I'd wait until Abe came up. My mom spoke ill of Roxanne, which shocked me because I was under the assumption she liked her; especially since we stayed in the same house.

"Baby, how are you?" Kasha asked and I turned my head to see who she was talking to.

Yes, I had a baby outside my relationship, my girl left me, took me back and I've been making it up to her ever since.

Roxanne couldn't accept Melody right now and I understood. I never forced her too either.

I know its hard being with someone who not only cheated but a child resulted in it. Roxanne loves kids and I know she would never hurt her but I can't expect her to raise another woman's child. I'm not sure had we broke up and she cheated, if I could do it either. She knows when I see Melody, and has even purchased her clothes, shoes and gifts for birthdays and holidays, which in my eyes is a start.

But what I can't figure out is why Melody's mom is here and she hasn't been in over three years. Is that why Roxanne isn't here? I know she shot me but I forgive her because what she walked in on is enough to make any woman snap from what Abe told me.

I was in a compromising position and it was eating me up on how I even got there. I'm always cautious with my drinks but Abe said in the video, it showed me switching seats for one of the women and at the same time another one dropped something in it. I asked why didn't it bubble or something. He told me it may have but I was so high and probably didn't pay attention. I had beef with no one to my knowledge so all of this was blowing my mind.

"Who you talking to?" I asked Kasha who tried kissing my lips.

"Bitch, are you crazy?" I pushed her head back with my good arm.

"Noah, don't speak to her like that. She's been here everyday while your other baby mama hasn't been up here to even say hello." My mom said.

"You know they say, you'll see who's there for you when something bad happens." Kasha's mom had the nerve to chime in.

"Yo, who asked you? And ma, why are you entertaining this shit? You know my girl won't be happy about this right here." I pointed to Kasha and her mom, but my mom waved me off.

"You're right she wouldn't be." I heard a voice and looked up to see Honor standing there with her face turned up. I lifted my bed up and waited for Roxanne to step in behind her but it never happened.

"I brought you some clothes and a few other things from your house. The rest will be put in storage along with all the furniture and anything else you have." Honor put a duffle bag next to me and kissed my cheek. She was my girl's best friend and like a sister to me.

Her facial expression told me something happened but its not the right time to mention it. She and I had a connection when it came to analyzing shit. No we were never sexually intimate or anything like that, we just clicked when it came to observing motherfuckers and picking out the grimy ones.

"Storage. Why are my things going in storage and where is Roxanne?" Honor stared at my mom and shook her head.

"Yooooo, your girl put your house up for sale." I heard Abe saying as he stepped in my room with his face in the phone.

"I'll see you later Noah and don't doubt the love she has for you because that will never change but right now she has to do what's best for the kids."

"What you mean what's best for my kids? What the fuck is going on?"

"Hey Honor. Can I talk to you for a minute?" Abe asked and she moved past him without speaking.

"What you mean my house is up for sale? Kasha what are you doing here and ma, what did you say to Roxanne? It has to be something if she packed up an left." Abe showed me a photo of the for sale sign sitting outside the house online. It wasn't much I could say about it because the house is in her name. As far as my mom goes, all she said is Roxanne is mad Kasha came to see me but that doesn't sound accurate either. How would my girl know that unless she told her?

"Noah, calm down. Your heart rate is speeding up and your pressure is jumping." Kasha's mom who is a nurse said listening to the machines go off.

"Abe, can you find my girl and kids? I need to see them and figure out what's going on? Roxanne wouldn't leave me up here like this and I know my kids miss me, hell, I'm missing them." He nodded his head and left. My mom rolled her eyes and Kasha sat next to her mom. Melody was on the bed with me coloring.

If anyone knew me, they were well aware of the relationship I had with my two older kids. Junior and Precious were with me all the time and were known everywhere. If my son were in the store with his friends acting up, someone would call me on the phone. If my daughter were getting smart with an adult or even her mom, I would get a phone call. There is no one out there who could ever tell you I wasn't in their life.

As far as my three year old, I was in hers as well but not as much. I saw her faithfully every weekend and during the week if I needed to. She stayed in a big house with her grandmother I paid for. It wasn't fair to have Kasha's mom taking care of my seed because she didn't want to. I am her father but I have to respect my girl's wishes as far as not bringing her around. It doesn't take away anytime from Melody and if she wanted me to stay the night with me, I had a condo for us.

My other kids didn't know of Melody and vice versa. My son is stubborn just like me, but he's a momma's boy. Don't get me wrong, he's no punk but that boy loves his mother. Now, my daughter Precious, she's daddy's girl and I can do no wrong in her eyes. She's spoiled as shit but she's supposed to be. Melody is still young but she gets everything she wants too.

I don't know what I'm going to do with three women in my life. I do know over the last few weeks, I've been trying to get my girl pregnant again. We wanted another baby and after the two she aborted before having our son, I knew she wouldn't do it again.

Roxanne assumed I didn't know about them but she was wrong. Like I said, everyone knew who I was and my girl too. Someone peeped her in the clinic but it was too late by the time I got there to stop her. She was walking out when I pulled up. I sat in the car and watched her cry as she sat on the bench waiting for a cab that came a short time after.

The second time, I only found out one night she went to the club with Honor. My mom stopped by and asked what some pills were when she came out the bathroom. I told her my girl had been sick so it most likely was from the doctor. She looked it up and they were the pills you take after terminating a pregnancy. I wanted to approach her but I left it alone.

When she got pregnant with my son I knew it because she was throwing up constantly. I gave her a ton of hints about killing any woman, who killed my kids. Two weeks later she told me about my son and a year and a half later we had my daughter. I told her if she didn't want any more kids right away to get on the pill and she did. Unfortunately, I messed around and got Kasha pregnant.

Kasha was something to do really and no feelings were involved on my end. I wore protection every time with her but the night she claimed to have gotten pregnant, she went down on me and right before I came; slammed down hard on my dick. It happened so quick I busted right away. A nigga was pissed and told her to get her shit.

When Roxanne caught us we had just stepped out the hotel from her revealing the pregnancy to me. She tried to run us over and even left me but I begged her to take me back and never stepped out on her again. It hurt her bad when I had to tell her about Kasha getting pregnant and how she kept it. I don't know if it hurt me more to tell her that or telling her the DNA confirmed me as the child's father. All in all, I hurt my girl and vowed to never do it again. That's why I didn't try to stop her when she pointed the gun at me. I saw hurt and pain on her face and I'm the one who put it there.

****

"Did you find them?" I asked Abe who came to pick me up from the hospital. I've been here for a month and still have yet to see my other kids. I didn't receive a phone call or a message from anyone.

"Nah. I thought she was with Honor but no one has been there but her."

"Hold on. You back with Honor?"

"Nah. She isn't giving me the time of day."

"How the hell you know where she stay?"

"Come on man."

"I don't even know why I asked." I laughed and let the nurse help me in the wheelchair. My arm was out of the sling but since she shot me in the forearm I had to wear a metal splint for another few weeks to keep the bone in place. As far as my chest, it healed quickly but every now and then I feel pain.

"What are you going to do now?" Abe asked and started the car.

"Right now, go lay down because this medicine is about to have me knocked out. I need you to pick me up tomorrow and take me by the house." I told him. I wanted to see if she left anything behind or still staying there. Honor told me she moved to keep me away but I wanted to see for myself.

"Alright yo. I'll get at you in the morning. Make sure you lock up. We don't want the big bad, baby mama from hell trying to rape you and have more kids."

"Fuck you nigga." I said and walked in my house.

Kasha had been at the hospital everyday begging me to make her my girl since Roxanne bounced. One... I never had a relationship with her and Melody was definitely an accident, and two... she neglected my daughter for three years. I could never be with a woman who chooses dick and money over her kid. Say what you want about my daughter not living with me but men do it all the time. As long as she is taken care of nobody's opinion matters to me. My mom tried to make me feel bad at the hospital too; talking about we need to be a family. That reminds me, I need to call her too. Something about the way she jumped on the Kasha bandwagon isn't sitting right with me.

I opened the door and there were boxes of my things piled up in the middle of the floor. All of it was labeled and they were stacked up neatly. One box in particular stood out. It was the big ass keepsake box I got for her after we got together years ago. She kept all the pictures of us on vacation, letters I wrote her just because, cards I gave her for birthdays, holidays and thinking of you ones. She wanted to have the box to read how I felt about her whenever she wanted to leave me. I opened it and on top of it was an envelope with my name on it.

I'm giving you this box to remember me. You will need it more than me. Where I'm going, it won't help me get over you. Goodbye Noah.

I tossed the box on the other side of the room and kicked over the ones in front of me. How dare she leave after she shot me? What the fuck is she thinking? Nah, she ain't leaving me, not now, not ever. First thing in the morning, I'm going to hire a private investigator to bring her back to me and we're going to work this out.

Honor

The night of Abe's homecoming party I was nervous when we walked in the club and it was live as fuck. When he approached me I got cold feet and didn't know what to do but leave; especially after Vera came over starting her nonsense. I can't lie though, Abe looked even better than before he went in. I wanted him in the worse way but things in my past kept me from moving forward sexually with him or any other man for that matter.

Now, I'm standing here staring into the face of a man who popped up at my house. He said since I've been avoiding him, he had to make sure I wouldn't run. I stepped aside and let him in. I stared as he made his way to the couch and patted a seat for me to sit next to him. I said a prayer to God for him to help me get through the night without having him inside me. He sat there leaned over on his knees, staring at me. His eyes could probably see straight through me and it would be my fault because under his gaze I felt naked as hell, right now. His tongue ran over his lips and a grin escaped.

"You scared of me now Honor?"

"No. I just don't see why you're here."

"It's been eleven years and I think its time for us to discuss what went down all those years ago."

"I don't want to." I tried to get up but he pulled me back down.

"Honor, stop running. I know I hurt you and a nigga is truly sorry. If I could take back the hurt I would but my daughter, I don't regret." I nodded my head.

"I admit I was young, dumb and trying to fuck anything in sight. I swear on everything that none of them meant anything to me, except Vera." I snapped my neck at him. He ran his hand down his face.

"Excuse me."

"Vera was there before you Honor and I did have love for her." I didn't say anything. These are things he should've told me prior to trying to wife me up.

"Vera and I were neighbors and each other's first." No wonder he couldn't stay away from her.

"Anyway, after we met and made you my girl, I left her alone. She went crazy and started making threats of killing herself unless she was my side chick." I gave him a weird look.

"I know, crazy right. I figured why not? You didn't know one another and she would be the one I got sex from. However, the longer I stayed with you, the harder she made it for me to keep her a secret. She hated seeing us out together or hearing people ask about you around me. Anything, having to do with you she had a problem with.

One day, I told her you and I broke up just so I could stop fucking her. Only thing is, she now wanted your spot but you were still there. I began sleeping around with other chicks trying to make her see I didn't want her but nothing worked. When she told me about her pregnancy, a nigga was sick. Honor, you were my heart and everyone on the streets knew it. I begged her to get rid of the baby up until the time passed where she could no longer have that as an option.

The day I told you and you cried, I couldn't sleep for days. Every time I closed my eyes, I saw you in the hospital bed screaming and crying your eyes out, asking me why didn't I wait for you. How could I hurt you that way?" I sat there listening.

"Vera kept the baby to spite you and the other women she assumed I was with. Honor, you were supposed to be the woman I married and gave my kids to. You were all the woman I needed and instead of coming clean in the beginning, I let shit escalate and lost you in the process." I wiped my eyes and stood up. He did the same and stared in my eyes.

"I'm sorry Honor. It doesn't make up for the hurt I caused you, but I hope it gives you closure on why I did it." I tried to respond but his lips were on mine and my arms were wrapped around his neck. My mouth opened and gave his tongue access to mine.

"I missed the fuck out of you Honor." He said when we stopped kissing.

"I missed you too Abe and its nice to see you but.-" He didn't let me finish, lifted me up and carried me to the bedroom.

"What are you doing?" I asked as he had me bend over on the bed. I felt his hands removing my pajama shorts and his tongue made its way to my bottom lips.

"Sssssss. Abe we shouldn't be." I whispered and jumped a little when his finger entered my dripping wet box. He maneuvered it, in and out and sucked on my clit at the same time. I've had my pussy ate before but never from the back and I'll be damned if I didn't feel like I've been missing out.

"Abe, I'm cumming." I felt my body succumbing to his mouth and screamed out as he made me reach an orgasm so hard; I fell on the bed and was ready to go to sleep.

"Nah baby. You're about to let me make love to you." He said removing his clothes.

"Abe, I'm not ready." I told him but it was a lie and he knew it. His mouth sucked on my nipples as his two hands cupped and massaged my breasts at the same time. The feeling was so damn good. He continued making my body feel good. I felt the tip at the entrance of my tunnel and became nervous.

"I got you Honor. Do you trust me?" I nodded my head. I'm not a virgin but after the tragic event I suffered, no man entered me so I may as well be.

"Tell me if it hurts too bad." He kissed me and pushed himself in slow and maneuvered in and out until he hit the bottom in which a bitch was in heaven by then.

"You ok Honor ?" At first I wasn't but if I dwelled on the pain, I'd never do it.

"I love you Honor. I never stopped." I began crying and he kissed each tear away.

"Abe, I'm cumming again." I moaned in his ear. He moved back, lifted my legs on his shoulders and told me to let him see. I covered my face laughing as he looked.

"Honor, this shit is sexy as fuck. Mmmmm." He bit on his lip, grunted and fell on the side of me. I turned over but he made me face him.

"I want you to be my woman."

"Abe right now we should be friends." He slipped his tongue in my mouth, pulled me on top of him and mounted me in a riding position. He spread my ass cheeks and slid me down. I tried to jump off but he caught me. He went deep and I felt a little pain. Abe isn't a little dick nigga at all and the width didn't make it any better.

"Go slow first and speed up when you're ready. Go at your own pace Honor." I did what he said and had his ass moaning. I began touching myself as I rode him and he said the sight had him even harder.

"I'm about to make love to you all night. You ok with that?" I didn't say anything as he pumped harder under me and made me cum two times in this position. He didn't lie about making love to me all night. After his first two nuts, he was like a machine but it felt good. I can't believe I waited this long but then again, I'm glad he's the one I chose to give my all too.

"I love you Abe." I whispered in his ear as he slept peacefully next to me. I won't say we're a couple yet but I don't plan on sleeping with anyone else. I hope he feels the same.

"You have to tell him where you are Roxanne." I had been seeing her every weekend and tried to get her to call Noah up. She was so damn bull headed and kept telling me no.

"No Honor and you better not either."

"I'm not. You know I wouldn't do that to you."

"How is he?" She asked me sadly.

"He's good Roxy. He doesn't understand why you left him or why he can't see his kids. Abe told me he hired a private investigator to find you. It's only a matter of time before he finds out and you know he's going to flip."

"When the person finds me, then I'll talk to him but not a minute before. I've heard about him and the other baby mama out in the open now. How could he do that to me Honor?"

"Hell no Roxy. You took him back after the baby so you don't get to be mad. If I were him, I'd be mad at you for not accepting his daughter."

"Honor, that's not fair."

61

"No it is Roxanne. I've kept quiet about it long enough. You took him back which meant you forgave him. The baby was made out of what he did and once he confirmed she was his, you should've taken her in too. I'm not saying you had to be her mom or have her sleeping over and shit like that, but you had a responsibility as his woman to step up to the plate. You have that man's child living with her grandmother because her mom didn't want her and her father has a woman who doesn't want to be bothered. Melody didn't ask to be here and it's not fair to her that she gets him part time while your kids get him full time."

"My kids were here first Honor and had he.-"

"Stop that shit Roxanne. Ok, he cheated, had a baby but who did he beg to take him back? You made him choose you over his child and that's fucked up. I love you Roxanne but in the last three years you have made a man you claim to love, love his child from a distance. You should've never taken him back." She started crying.

"You would be ok if Abe brought his daughter around you?"

"Yes and no. I say no because she is a constant reminder that he cheated and hurt me. But at the same time, I would be ok with her because she had nothing to do with the irresponsible choice he made. I can't punish her for what he did. The minute I took him back, I took the kid with me."

"Honor, he hurt me so bad having another child." I sat next to her.

"Roxanne, I know he did. I'm not saying you don't have the right to feel the way you do but Melody has a right to know her siblings and her father full time. I understand the kids are mad but had you told them sooner, the impact from their hateful ass grandmother wouldn't have hit them as hard. Kids forgive faster than adults but when you wait to tell them things, that should've been told to them a while ago, it affects them different."

"Maybe we should stay away from each other you know. Let him be in Melody's life and get the kids when he wants too. I don't have to be with him to take care of his kids."

"I'll support whatever choice you make but before you make that hasty decision you need to speak with him first.

You're being unfair to everyone involved right now because you're hurt."

"How's it going with you and Abe?" She changed the subject and I'm ok with that because we needed to lighten the mood.

"We're good. Taking it one day at a time though." Its been two months since he asked me to be his woman and so far, so good. No one really knows yet, but I'm sure once his baby mama finds out all hell is going to break loose.

"Have you met bad ass Chelsea yet?" I smiled.

"Yes and she is a sweetheart." She turned her face up.

"We can't be speaking of the same kid."

"Chelsea is a good kid. She is dealing with a lot when it comes to Vera. You know her dad has been locked up for a long time and the entire time Vera fed her lies about him not wanting her and whoever his girlfriend is wouldn't like her and a bunch of other shit. I told Abe about one conversation Chelsea and I had and he was ready to kill Vera. Now, he doesn't know shit and I'm not telling unless it's really bad."

"He's very protective of her and you."

"Me!"

"Yes you. He had people watching over you the entire time he was on locked down." I smiled. I had no idea of the impact I had on him.

"Time's up Miss Paul." I heard the officer say. She gave me a hug and watched me walk out the room like she always did.

"Here are your things Honor. Will we see you next week?" The girl in the front asked. I had been seeing her three days a week for the last three months. She and I were on a first name basis.

"Same time, same place. Have a good weekend." I told her and walked outside. I turned my phone on and made my way to my car. I started reading the messages and bumped into someone.

"You better tell me right now who the fuck you're visiting in jail before I break your neck." Abe said to me with enough venom in his voice to kill me off that alone.

"No one and we're not together like that." I moved past him and he yoked me up by the back of my shirt.

"Don't play with me Honor. I love you but I swear if you're fucking someone else, I'll get over your death one day." I looked in his eyes and became scared all of a sudden.

"I'm scared to tell you."

"You got five seconds to open your mouth." He stared at me.

"Roxanne." He let my shirt go, looked at the jail, back at me and repeated it. He left me standing there and walked over to my car. She is going to kill me but I had no choice. I wasn't losing my life to keep her secret.

"Mommy can we get a gift for daddy? I called grandma and she said he was in the hospital sick." Me and my son stared at her. Noah had gotten her a metro PCS phone to call him whenever she wanted to talk to him. She was daddy's little girl and right now I hated it.

"When did grandma tell you this?" I asked as we walked through the grocery store. I stopped and surveyed my surroundings.

"What's wrong ma?" My son knew me like a book. He must've caught me being paranoid. I had been since shooting Noah but Abe told me he had the tape so no one knew I did it.

"Did your sister put anything in her pocket?" I asked as some man entered every aisle we did. Usually it meant they were from loss prevention and saw you on the screen taking something.

"Not this time. I've been next to her the entire time." He stared at me and I hugged him.

"Junior, I'm going to tell you something and I want you to answer me with a head nod and whatever you do, do not look around in the store." He nodded his head.

"There is a man following us. I'm not sure why but when we get to the car you know where it is right?" He nodded knowing I spoke of my gun. Noah took him to the gun range a few times despite me asking him not too. He showed him all about guns and right now I'm happy he did.

We continued shopping and just like I thought, a man continued entering every aisle as us. Precious didn't have a clue but my son did. I had to stop him a few times from saying something. I swear he thinks he's older than his age. I stood in the checkout line with the kids pretending everything was ok. The moment we stepped outside a woman approached me and showed her badge.

"I'm a mother before anything and I promise nothing is going to happen in front of your kids." I nodded my head.

"You're going to get in your car, drive home and make a call to someone who can pick them up."

"Ma, are you ok?" Precious asked.

"Yes baby. Call nana and see if she's home." Nana is my mom and who we resided with at the moment. It had been a few days since I shot Noah and I moved us out the house quickly. I wanted to get out before I murdered his mother.

"What is this about?" I told Junior to get in the car after he helped me put the groceries in the car.

"I will tell you when we get to your house." I didn't say anything.

"Nana's home. She said hurry up though because she needs the stuff to make the spaghetti."

"Thank you." I told the detective. She stepped away and got in her car. I pulled out the parking lot and saw three cars do the same. I guess if I planned to speed they had me trapped but that will never happen with my babies in the car. We got to my moms and I had the kids bring the groceries inside.

"Ma, this is Ms. Mendez." Instantly my mom knew something was up and sent the kids to their rooms.

"What is this about?" My mom asked wiping her hands on the paper towels.

"Miss Paul is being charged with the attempted murder of Noah Boone and shooting into a crowd of people." My mom told the officer she understood and so did I but who told on me? I know Abe didn't and I don't know the women who were in the room with him or the people at the house.

"Ma'am you have the right to remain silent. Anything you say, can and will be held against you in the court of law." As she ran my rights down and placed the handcuffs on me, Junior came running down the steps trying to attack the male officers. Precious had no idea what was happening and started screaming.

"Ms. Mendez, I know its asking for a lot but please give me a minute with my kids." She and the other officers stepped outside. I bent down in front of my kids who were hysterical crying.

"Junior, I need you to take care of your sister. Don't let your other grandmother treat her anyway or make her feel like I don't love her." He nodded his head with tears coming down his face.

"Mommy, don't let them take you." Precious grabbed my neck and wouldn't let go.

"Ma, can you get her please?" She would not let go.

"Junior you are the man of the house. Take care of nana and when I leave, take it out my car and put it in the safe. Precious can't know about it."

"What did you do ma?" I stood up and went to walk outside where the officers were waiting.

"I tried to kill your father for hurting me." I knew he wouldn't understand but I'll explain it later. The woman officer pushed my head down to get in the car and I watched my kids stand at the door with my mom crying while I met my fate.

The next day, I went to court to stand in front of the judge to hear the charges against me. Honor, my mom and son were there. I begged my mom not to bring him but I see she couldn't keep him away. I begged them not to inform anyone; especially Noah's mom or Abe. I committed the crime and I had to deal with my consequences. That was three months ago and I've been here everyday waiting on sentencing. I didn't ask *for a lawyer nor did I admit to anything. I would deal with it all on my own.*

After Honor left, I thought a lot about what she said when it came to Noah and she was right. I should've never accepted him back and the baby didn't deserve to have him part time. I made plans to call him tomorrow after my visit with the kids. I had to talk to them and have their father come see them. It's not fair to keep him away when I'm the one who almost killed him. I went to sleep writing him another letter like I did every night telling him how I felt. I had so many but never sent them because I didn't want him to know where I was.

****

"Miss Paul, you have a visitor." The correction officer told me. I glanced up at the clock and it was only ten in the morning. My mom wasn't supposed to show up for another hour. Knowing Precious she had her up at the crack of dawn. They didn't like where I was but I explained to them that what I did was wrong and had to deal with the decision I made. I wanted my kids to know you can't get away with trying to kill

72

someone, even if they hurt you. I never want to see them in a jail. I'm hoping this is a learning experience for them.

"I'm ready." I checked my self over as usual. I always tried to look presentable regardless of this brown uniform. My mom sent me a pair of white air macs for my feet and Honor made sure I had money on my commissary for food, pads and personal hygiene products.

"How are mommy's babies?" I asked when the door to the room opened. My eyes got big as hell when I saw Noah standing there. I attempted to turn around but the correction officer shut the door and shrugged her shoulders. *Did this bitch know he was here?*

"Sit down Roxanne." He said in a voice telling me not to defy him. I took a seat away from him and he pulled a chair up in front of me.

"Why didn't you call me?" He asked and I immediately broke down when I noticed my name freshly tatted on his neck. How could I try to kill a man who loved me? He stood me up and hugged me. I broke down harder in his arms. I don't know how long we were like that but when I pulled away I saw a few tears in his eyes.

"I'm sorry Noah for almost killing you. Your phone called me with a woman yelling out your name, I tracked you and walked in on you having sex with those women. I snapped and... and... I'm so sorry. My kids almost lost their father and I'm in jail for trying to kill you. What have I done?"

"Roxanne, I forgave you for what went down. I don't blame you for it. I can't imagine what went through your head and you always told me you would kill me if I cheated on you again. I believed you and even if I didn't, I damn sure do now." We both laughed. He stepped in the bathroom and came out with tissues.

"Noah, I'm sorry too for making you sacrifice being in Melody's life part time. I was wrong and neither you nor her deserved that. The kids have been with my mom so whenever you want to get them, they'll be there."

"I miss the hell out of my kids and you too. Why are you speaking as if you won't be released?"

"I didn't ask for a lawyer and.-"

74

"None of that matters. I already have someone on your case. You'll be out of here by the end of the week."

"Noah, I have to face my consequences."

"No you don't. I forgave you and its not up to the system to decide if I should or not, meanwhile letting you rot in here. That's not ok for my woman." I smiled when he called me his woman.

"DADDYYYYYYY!" I heard a voice yell out. Precious ran over and gave him a big hug. Junior stood off to the side. My mom gave him a hug and told how she's been telling me to call him. I gestured for my son to sit next to me but when he did, he kept his head down.

"Junior, you're not going to speak?" Noah asked and I felt my son tense up. He blamed his father for everything.

"What for? You're the reason my mom is in here."

"What motherfucker?" Noah yoked his ass up quick as hell.

"Ma, take Precious in the bathroom or out in the yard please."

"Noah, relax and put him down.

"No. This nigga wants to blame me so let me hear why he thinks that. Come on, you tough. Talk that shit now."

"Noah, he's nine, not twenty."

"Well he shouldn't run his mouth like a grown man and I wouldn't treat him like one." Noah let him go and sat down in front of me waiting for Junior to speak.

"You're the reason my mom is in jail because you cheated on her. Now, we have a sister from some other woman when my mom is the only one who is suppose to have your kids. You made my mom weak dad, and now look. She couldn't take it, tried to kill you and we haven't had her in three months because of you. I don't care what you say, you are the reason my mom was taken from us." I saw hurt on Noah's face. Junior wasn't disrespectful as he spoke because like I stated before, he's scared to death of his father.

"Who told you that?"

"Your mother when she told my mom, she wished it was her in the hospital and hoped she died." He looked at me and I shrugged my shoulders.

"Junior, you're right. It is my fault she's in here and I can't apologize enough for it. However, I had no idea she was here because she would have never spent one night behind bars. My lawyer is working on getting her out now but because she's been here for a while it may take a few days but she'll be home soon. Damn, I fucked up again Roxanne." I didn't say anything.

"I'm going to leave because I can see this is a family moment and I'm no longer a part of it."

"Noah, that's not fair. You are their father and they're hurting. I tried to shield them as long as I could but your mom."

"Don't blame all this on her Roxanne. Yes, what she said about you and how she disclosed the information to my son is wrong and I'm going to deal with that soon as I get home. But you had a part in this too. I told you when we first found out to mention it to the kids but you said it wasn't the right time and now look." Junior looked at me in shock.

"My mom told him in a fucked up way I'm sure, and my son felt he could come for me over it. Roxanne, I love you with all my heart God knows I do but we need to separate. I can't do this anymore. I know you're not comfortable with Melody and I would never force her on you. Now that everything is out in the open, all my kids will have me full time." I didn't say anything. I wanted to fight to stay together but he was right. This was partly my fault.

"I'll be over to get my kids tomorrow." He told my mom and she shook her head.

"Junior, if you don't want to come I understand and I'll give you a pass but you will get over it."

"Dad, I don't want to be around her."

"Who?"

"The baby's mother."

"Junior, she and I aren't a couple and I would never put you or your sister in that situation. Shit, I don't even want to be around her." Junior started laughing and so did Noah. He got up and gave his father a hug and apologized for being rude.

"I'm proud of you son. You had your mom's back even if it was to me. Never allow any man or woman to treat her anyway." He kissed his forehead and Precious on the cheek.

"Let me talk to you real quick Roxanne." I stood up and walked to the door. He lifted my chin and stared in my eyes.

"The lawyer should have you out of here soon. I know your mom has the kids but you will have a house and a car when you get out."

"Noah no. I don't want you to." He pecked my lips.

"Us not being together means nothing Roxanne. In my heart you are mine and we're taking a break right now. That's all. I have a lot to handle right now with my mom too. Melody's grandmother and mother are trying to get custody and I'm not having it. She left her once and I'm not taking the chance on it happening again. I also need to find out who had those women drug me and why?"

"Noah, do what you need to. This is what we both need. We've been together so long that maybe its good to see other people."

"Is that what you want? I said taking a break, not seeing other people." He looked hurt.

"I'm saying Noah."

"Is that what you want?" I shrugged my shoulders. He nodded his head and yanked the door open so hard it hit the wall and put a hole in it. I didn't want anyone else but I felt like if he heard it, he would move on and be happy. *I guess not.*

These past couple of months have been nothing but pure bliss for me. I had Abe to fulfill my sexual needs, but I still wouldn't call him my man yet. We haven't had a lot of sex but we sure had enough. Vera has been a bitch lately and for some reason I felt like she had something up her sleeve. I didn't trust her as far as I could see. She's always wanted to be number one in Abe's life and since she can't, I'm positive she's going to try something. I guess when he was in jail she didn't care because no one could have him but he's out now and she's up to her old tricks, I'm sure.

"Thank you for doing my hair." Chelsea said standing up out the chair.

"Anytime baby cakes, now come on, and let's go so I can take you by your mom's."

"Awe man." She pouted and that tore me up inside. She usually didn't go with Vera anymore but Abe was busy and I told him I'd take her to get some clothes.

"Don't be like that, it's just for a few minutes."

"Ok." She replied with her mouth but her face said something totally different.

We pulled up in front of her moms' house and I noticed quite a bit of cars. Chelsea looked at me and it didn't take a rocket scientist to see she wanted to leave. I undid my seatbelt and went on her side to open the door. She stepped out and grabbed my hand to go in. You could hear music blasting and there were people coming from around the back.

I smelled weed and food mixed together but what I didn't need to smell was the stench coming from in the house. I called out for Vera but like I said the music was loud. We walked though the kitchen and the bathroom door was opened and some woman had her arm out, shooting something in it. Another person was in the kitchen cooking something on the pot and when I looked it was white. I'm assuming it was crack.

"Excuse me. Have you seen Vera?" I asked some woman who passed a blunt to the chick next to her.

"She was upstairs with her baby daddy." I immediately got mad and took off up there to see if it were true. Chelsea held my hand in hers and even though the sight may not have been one for her to see, I damn sure wasn't about to leave her with these people. I checked her room and told her to get some clothes and put them in a bag. I closed her door and walked to the room she pointed to as her moms.

"Right there baby. Shitttttt. I'm going to cum." You could hear who I'm expecting to be Vera moaning. The door was unlocked and I wasn't about to stand there thinking if I should look or not. I walked right in and let my breath out I held in, when I noticed it was some other chick riding the hell out of some guy. I eased back out and shut the door before they saw me.

"Did you enjoy the show ma?" I turned around and this guy was beautiful, if I say so myself. He was tall, dark skin with perfect teeth and his body was impeccable. His jeans hung off his waist and the shirt accentuated his muscles.

"I'm sorry. I walked in the wrong room." I tried to move past him but he blocked me.

"What's your name sexy?" He licked those sexy ass lips, glancing over my body.

"Honor and yours?" I crossed my arms and leaned back on the wall. I had no business entertaining him when I had a man.

"Honor huh? I like that."

"I'm ready." Chelsea came out the room saving me from the stare down he and I were having.

"Hey lil mama. I didn't know you were here."

"Uncle Ernestttttt." She jumped in his arms and kissed his cheeks.

"I missed you." He said and put her down and placing fifty dollars in her hand.

"That is too much money for her."

"She good. Why is my niece with you?"

"You're Vera's brother?" I got an instant attitude. Anyone affiliated with her would never be affiliated with me.

"Yea so." He held my arm and Chelsea ran down the steps to go see his daughter he just told her was there.

"So. Your sister and I don't get along and I was bringing Chelsea to get clothes and see her but with all these people and illegal activities going on, it's best we leave." He pushed me against the wall and stood there.

"Ugh excuse me."

"Are you the one her punk ass baby daddy cheated on her with?" I pushed him back.

"He didn't cheat on her with me but I am the one he cheated on with her."

"Whatever happened, he played both of you. I can see why he wanted you though."

"Why is that and can I go please?"

"Nah, not yet." He grabbed me in the bathroom and locked the door. I prayed he wasn't about to rape me.

"Aren't you the woman who gets paid for a nigga to taste the pussy?"

"What? No, I'm not." I felt him messing around the button on my jeans. He had me fucked all the way up thinking some shit like that.

"I think you are." He stuck his hand in my jeans and began flickering my pearl. I shouldn't have been enjoying his touch but I did. Abe and I had sex but we weren't a couple yet.

What I was allowing this unknown man to do isn't cheating, is it?

I felt him tugging my jeans down with his free hand and in seconds he had me stepping out of them and my panties as he sat me on the sink with my legs gapped open. He got on his knees and gave my bottom lips pecks. I could feel his breath as he entered two fingers and let me fuck them as if it were his dick. My pearl began to get hard and his mouth sucked on my nub and I was almost at my peak.

"ERNEST are you in there?" I heard who someone ask who sounded like Vera.

"Fuckkkkk we have to stop." I whispered as my legs shook.

"When you cum I will." He stared at me and seconds later I exploded. He stood up and his dick was hard as hell poking in his jeans. He undid them and let his boxers fall and it took everything in me not to laugh. His dick was little and that's not the only problem. His ass wasn't circumcised.

"Suck it." He said stroking it.

"What? Hell no." I started putting my panties on and then my jeans. I got one leg in and he grabbed me by the waist.

"Let go Ernest." He was kissing up my back through my shirt, which is weird. I was able to get my other leg in my jeans and my flip-flops on. I jumped up and buttoned them.

"Come on Honor. Don't do me like that."

"Ernest, I didn't ask you to go down on me, nor did I promise to return the favor. I'm sorry if you thought that but I'm seeing someone."

"Come here." He grabbed me harder and sat me on his lap and tried grinding my lower half on him.

"Get off Ernest." I stood up and he did the same.

"Get the fuck over here." He snatched me by the hair and smacked me so hard I fell to the floor.

"I can't believe you hit me." I tried to stand but he punched me this time and I passed out. When I woke up he was kneeled over in front of me, pumping his dick in and out my mouth moaning. I pushed him off and he fell back.

"Dammit Honor. I was almost there."

"Stay the fuck away from me." I kicked him in his balls over and over. He cried out for me to stop but I didn't care. I unlocked the door and opened it, only to find Vera standing out there with a smirk on her face.

"I guess my baby daddy isn't doing his job, if you're here fucking my brother."

"Trust me, your baby daddy handles my body just fine but something is seriously wrong with your brother. You need to get him some help. And we never had sex."

"There's nothing wrong with him."

"Yea, well him punching me in the face and raping my mouth as I'm knocked out, would qualify him as having something wrong."

"Bitch, what did you do to my brother?" She asked after running in the bathroom. I took off downstairs and ran to find Chelsea who was sitting there with another kid. I snatched her hand and ran to the car crying. Yes, its my fault I allowed the man to eat my pussy but him forcing himself in my mouth is not right, I don't care what anyone says.

"What happened to your face Honor? You're bleeding and you have white stuff on your face." *Did this nigga nut on me?*

"I'm ok Chelsea. Let me get you to your grandmothers. Do me a favor and don't mention this to anyone please."

"Did my uncle Ernest do it? He hurts all the women and my mom said he should have never been released from jail."

"JAIL!" I yelled out scaring her.

"Yea. It was his coming home party. Maybe you should have grandma look at your face since she's a nurse."

"Its ok Chelsea. I'm going to the doctors after I drop you off." The rest of the ride we were both quiet. I could tell she wanted to ask me more questions but didn't. I pulled up at her grandmas and waited for her to get out.

"I'm sorry he hurt you Honor but please don't stop coming to get me." She gave me a hug and got out the car. I pulled off crying and almost got in two accidents because my eyes were blurry. I sent a text to Abe and told him I wasn't feeling well and I would see him tomorrow.

I took a boiling hot shower, brushed my teeth and rinsed my mouth a thousand times. I took some cotton balls, doused them with alcohol and cleaned my face with it. I sat in my bed thinking about what went down and became disgusted with myself. Yea, its partly my fault but how could I tell anyone without them thinking differently of me? I laid there until I fell asleep. Today was a depressing day, but one thing I know for sure; Abe is the only man who will ever touch my body from here on out.

****

I opened my eyes the next day and there was my man asleep next to me. I saw his morning wood sticking up and wanted nothing more than to sit on it. Ever since he introduced me to sex; I've become addicted. I yawned and it felt like my mouth was swollen. I ran in the bathroom and almost screamed when I saw my face. I had a few blisters on my mouth and one or two on the side of my cheek. They looked like cold sores but I couldn't tell. I tried to touch it but was scared of spreading.

I peeked in the room and Abe was still asleep. I threw on some sweats, a t-shirt and some sneakers and ran out the house and took an Uber to the emergency room. I went to send him a message and realized I left my phone home. I was now in the hospital alone and embarrassed. It felt like I was under a microscope when really no one paid me any mind. After running a few tests the doctor came in the room with another woman and closed the door. I was nervous because she looked like someone who would take my kids away if I had any.

"Hi Miss Chestnut. I'm Nancy Jones and I am the social worker here at the hospital. I'm here for moral support and to answer any questions you may have once the doctor gives you the information."

"Ummm ok."

"Miss Chestnut, all your blood work came back fine but we have two things we need to discuss with you." I sat up in the bed.

"The blisters on your face and lips are considered "Oral Herpes." I covered my mouth and then dropped my hand when I realized it was herpes.

"You have these on your face as well as quite a bit inside your mouth. Did you recently have oral sex with someone?"

"Kind of."

"What do you mean kind of?" Miss Nancy asked. I explained to them what happened as far as him hitting me and what he was doing when I woke up.

"The man may have been infected with genital herpes and most likely had an outbreak. Unfortunately, he spread it to you and it's going to take at least week or two of medication to get rid of it. You may not see any reoccurring symptoms because it isn't in your vaginal area but it's known to come back in clusters, such as what you are experiencing now." I nodded my head to let him know I understood.

"The other issue we came across is that you are pregnant." The nurse brought in an ultrasound machine as he said it and he performed an internal exam. His facial expression changed as he removed the tool from inside me and dipped it in the bucket.

"I'm sorry to tell you this but the baby is in your tubes. It's known as an ectopic pregnancy. Unfortunately, the child won't survive and it's in your best interest to terminate the pregnancy as soon as possible." I found myself hysterical crying. He left me alone with the lady who sat next to me.

"Miss Chestnut what happened to you is unfortunate but you know the law considers what he did to you as rape."

"I can't say anything. The guy I'm seeing doesn't know what happened and I don't want to lose him." She stood up and closed the door the doctor left open and asked me to explain everything that happened in full detail.

"I see." She sat opposite of me and took my hands in hers.

"Honey, just because you allowed him to taste your sweetness, doesn't give him the right to do that. The man obviously has problems but I understand your concern. However, we need to deal with this pregnancy and get you treated for what he gave you. Do you need me to contact anyone?"

"I want to call him because I know he's worried about me but I can't let him see me like this."

"I don't agree with you not informing him of the pregnancy, however, its not much he can do and I'll respect your wishes. I'm going to get the doctor back in here to go over everything pertaining to the surgery." I told her thank you. She left me her card and said she would check up on me tomorrow.

The doctor told me he could perform the surgery first thing in the morning and its best to stay the night. I laid back in the bed and cried until I couldn't cry anymore. I contracted a disease from a man who thought it was ok to violate me and on top of that I had to terminate a pregnancy I had no idea about. What else could go wrong?

"Yes, my brother needs help. A woman attacked him yesterday in the groin area and he hasn't been able to use the bathroom." I heard Vera yelling out at the nurses' station. I guess God is punishing me.

Abe

I rolled over in the bed and noticed Honor was missing. I went in the bathroom to handle my hygiene and see what she was cooking. Every morning she'd make me breakfast and let me sex her down anywhere I wanted. I came out searching the apartment and she wasn't anywhere in sight nor did she cook. I picked my cell up to call her but I heard the phone ringing on the nightstand. It isn't like Honor to leave her phone. I saw she had a few calls from someone whose number wasn't logged in. I assumed it to be Roxanne since she wasn't home yet. I started putting my clothes on and my phone rang.

"What up?"

"Hey baby daddy." I rolled my eyes listening to her tell me she saw my girl at her house yesterday.

"Vera she was bringing Chelsea to get clothes."

"Yea right. I think you need to come see what I have to show you."

"You know damn well I'm not coming to your house." I hung the phone up and got my shit together to go see if Honor was at my mom's. She had become tight with my mom now that we were together. She's still saying we're not a couple but everyone knows that's my woman. Years ago my mom always told me Honor was the one for me but being young and dumb I didn't take heed to what she said. Who knew all these years later she would be right?

I locked the door and walked to my car, which was parked next to hers. Instantly bad thoughts began to invade my head. Honor didn't have her phone or her car, yet, she wasn't in the house. I hit Noah up and asked him to meet me over my mom's. Honor has been known to disappear but now that we're on good terms I'm not sure why she'd do it now.

I got to my mom's and saw Chelsea on the porch playing with her cousins. As soon as she saw me, she ran up and jumped in my arms. She looked around me and asked where Honor was and if she were ok. I put her down and asked what she meant but Chelsea said she promised not to tell. I respected it because the two of them were close too.

"Have you seen Honor?" My mom asked coming out the bedroom in her robe.

"No. I woke up this morning and she was gone. I assumed she would be here or at work but her car is still at the house."

"Chelsea told me when she went to her moms yesterday Honor got hurt but she wouldn't tell me how? I tried all night to get it out of her but her lips were sealed."

"Hurt how? I stayed the night with her and she seemed fine but then again I got there late and she was asleep."

"I don't know but Chelsea has been asking for her all morning." I nodded my head and glanced down at my phone ringing again. It was this chick name Monica I hit off a few times when I first came home and Honor wouldn't have anything to do with me. I sent her to voicemail as usual and listened to my mom.

Once I had sex with Honor she became my woman regardless of her saying we needed to go slow. I may have slept with other chicks but make no mistake that Honor is mine and always will be. I'm dropping everyone when she accepts her spot as my woman.

"What's up aunty?" Noah said kissing my mom on the cheek and speaking to me before grabbing a bowl and pouring cereal in it.

"Nothing fool. Why haven't I seen my grandbabies and what's this about a new kid you had outside of Roxy?"

"Who told you?"

"You know Chelsea and Precious are best friends. They tell each other everything." He began explaining to my mom what happened and she punched him in the chest.

"Aunty, really?"

"Yes really? You know how much Roxy loved you. How could you step out on her like that? Before you say it, I don't agree with how she handled making you choose her or the baby but I understand."

"Roxy is the only one I want but she couldn't move past what I did and instead of leaving me alone she stayed."

"Love makes us do crazy things but you didn't have to stay either. Once she gave you the ultimatum, you had the opportunity to walk away as well. I blame both of you for the foolery. And now she's in jail over the bullshit."

"I know and she never would have been had she not kept her incarceration to herself. Aunty, I swear I put a lawyer on it and she should be out in a few days."

"She better be or me and you are going to have more problems. Now if you'll excuse me, my man, your daddy, needs me." She pointed to me laughing.

"Yo, I'm out before I get nauseous."

"What? Pretty soon both of you will be my age and your kids will say the same."

"Whatever." My mom shut the door and I heard the music turn on. At least they had the decency to do that with the kids outside.

"You think something happened to Honor?" Noah asked stuffing the spoon in his mouth.

"I don't know. She was there last night and bounced this morning. You know she be on her disappearing act sometimes." I told him and he nodded his head.

"Alright yo. I'll see you later. I'm about to see what the fuck Monica wants."

"Your girl missing and you're going to see the side piece." He asked shaking his head in disappointment.

"Honor said she didn't want me as her man right now so it is what it is." We slapped hands and I headed out. I gave Chelsea money because my sister was taking her and the other kids to fun time America.

****

"Suck that shit Monica. Ahhhh fuckkkk." I moaned out as my toes curled. Monica had a lethal head game and whenever she offered I couldn't resist. I initially came over to tell her we were taking a break because of her being clingy but here I am with my dick down her throat.

"Damn girl. You know how to suck some dick." She wiped her mouth and disappeared; coming back with a brand new box of condoms. I don't play that single wrapper shit; if the box is open or tampered with, I refused to use them. She opened one, rolled it down and slid down on my pole and her pussy sucked all of me up.

"Oh shit Abe. Fuck this dick is good." Monica bounced up and down as she buried her face in my neck trying to stop herself from yelling.

The way she sucked and kissed on my neck had me harder. I grabbed on her hips and thrusted under her. She continued moaning and calling out my name. I stopped, turned her over and hit it from behind. She didn't have a huge ass but it was enough for me to squeeze. I told her to throw it back and home girl did it so good I had to stop myself from cumming fast. She and I fucked for a while and fell on the floor breathing hard.

"I can never get enough of this dick." She said and grabbed him again in attempt to wake him up.

"Yea well, if you don't stop being so fucking clingy, you won't ever get this again." She kissed my cheek, then my chest. I felt her about to go down when my phone rang.

"What?" It was Vera again.

"Check your phone. I sent you something."

"Damnnnnnn. Shitttttt." I moaned when Monica took me in her mouth.

"Abe."

"What Vera, damn? I'll look when ole girl finish sucking my dick." I heard her suck her teeth as I hung up. Monica did her thang and I rewarded her with more dick. A few times she's asked me to go down on her but unless her name is Honor, it will never happen.

I washed up in the bathroom and came out to see Monica sitting on the couch looking at her phone. Monica is definitely a pretty woman but she isn't Honor. She was a red bone with a nice body but not the stripper kind. She worked at a bank, had her own place and could fuck me all night if I wanted her to. We both had stamina for days but she wanted a relationship and I couldn't give her that right now. Maybe, if I weren't building with Honor she could get it. I looked at my phone and it dawned on me that Vera sent something. I hated to open it being she's been sending me nude photos or videos of her pleasuring her self and calling out my name all the time.

"What the fuck?" I yelled out and Monica looked up at me.

"Are you ok?" She asked. I kissed her cheek and told her I would see her later. I ran by Vera's house and banged on the door. Or course, she opened it half naked.

"Where did you get this from?" I asked of the video and pictures she sent. The photos were of Honor's eyes closed on the floor with a dick in her mouth and the video was her actually sucking his dick.

"Someone sent it to me."

"Who the fuck is the guy?"

"I don't know who he is and why should it matter? That's the so-called love of your life giving head to someone else. I thought she was the type of chick who allowed people to do her, not the other way around." She had a smirk on her face.

"Whoever he is, is a dead man when I find him." She looked nervous like she knew who the person was.

"How you mad at the dude?"

"Because a real man isn't going to spread a video of what he does with a woman. You can see her eyes closed, which means she had no idea he was taping her. In my eyes, he violated all around. As far as her, don't ever worry about what

103

the fuck she has going on." I slammed the door and walked out. Now I was really mad Honor disappeared. But you can bet when I find her, I'm going to have a lot to say.

****

Three days went by and I still hadn't heard or seen Honor anywhere. I stayed at her house at night but she never showed up and during the day I had someone outside waiting to call me if she did. This morning I went by my moms to see if she had spoken to her and she didn't. Where the fuck was this chick and how the hell is she hiding so good? I wonder if she knows I'm aware of the video but then again she's no punk and wouldn't give a fuck.

"Who this?" I answered my phone without looking.

"Abe."

"Honor is that you?" I heard some sniffling on the phone.

"Yes."

"Where the fuck have you been?"

"I'm in the hospital."

"Hospital."

"Yes. I'm on the fourth floor."

"I'll be right there." She didn't say anything and hung up. I raced up there because no matter how mad I was, anything could've been wrong. I walked in her room and some lady was sitting on the bed talking to her. I heard her saying she had to tell me.

"Honor." She looked up and I wanted to throw up. Her face had some sores on it and they were disgusting.

"What the hell happened to you?"

"I'll leave you alone." The woman closed the door.

"Is this where you've been?" I asked looking around the room.

"Yes."

"Why didn't you call me?"

"Abe I didn't know how to tell you what happened?"

"Oh you mean this." I pulled my phone out and showed her the video and photos. She started crying and shaking.

"Where did you get that? Abe, you have to believe me when I say it's not what it looks like."

"Oh it isn't. It damn sure looks like you giving some nigga head." I saw her give me a hard stare and shake her head.

"You know what? Maybe, you should go."

"Why? Huh? Because this nigga got you on video and probably sent the shit out to everyone we know?" She tossed the covers back and came to where I stood and smacked the shit out of me.

"No. I want you to leave because I called you here to explain what happened and why I'm really here but you waltz your trifling ass up in here with two fucking hickeys on your neck."

"Honor."

"Honor my ass motherfucker. I said I wasn't ready for a relationship with you and this is why? This is the same shit you did to me years ago. You couldn't wait for me, so you went out and fucked whomever until I gave you my answer. Am I right?" I didn't say anything.

"Exactly. While you were out fucking the next bitch, I was here getting prepped to terminate our baby."

"WHAT?"

"Yea. I've been calling you for the last three days but either your phone was off or you wouldn't answer. Our baby was in my tubes and it was no way for them to save it. I needed you here by my side but you couldn't do it because you were fucking the next chick." She was crying as she got back in the bed.

"This is exactly why I didn't want to be with you. You are so fucking selfish and whoever she is, can have your ass. I'm done with you. Don't call my phone, don't stop by my house and do us both a favor and stay the fuck away from me. I mean I'm a whore who just allowed any man to stick his dick in my mouth right."

"Honor."

"Abe, I haven't even gone down on you. How could you think I would do it to someone else."

"I thought."

"What you thought, because I let a few men eat my pussy over the years, it means I do the same? Well it doesn't and for you to think of me in that way goes to show, you see me the same as everyone else." She never had sex with men but during the time she may have been seeing someone, she'd let him go down on her and I did think she returned the favor.

"What do you want me to think Honor? Did you see the video?"

"Yea, I saw it but you still haven't asked me what went down. And when did you get it?"

"The other day, why?"

"The other day, huh?" I shook my head yes.

"Those hickeys are fading, which means you fucked that woman before you saw the video. Get out Abe."

"So what Honor. She don't.-" She stopped me.

"Yes she does. Just like you told me Vera didn't mean shit, this woman means something. You allowed her to leave marks on your body and I know you Abe. In the short amount of time we've slept together, you've told me, you only allow a woman you're feeling to leave hickeys on you. You feel like, how did you say it, *"She's letting women know you're taken."* I let my hand run over my head.

"I guess she's letting me know too."

"It was an accident Honor. You are the only woman."

"STOP IT ABE PLEASE! I CAN'T TAKE THE LIES."

"Honor this isn't over." I went to leave.

"Yes it is. I fucking hate you." I stopped and turned to look at her. My heart sunk in my chest as I saw her roll up in a fetal position and let out a gut-wrenching scream. How could I do her like that after everything she's been through? A nurse and the woman, who was there when I came, ran in the room asking if she was ok.

I left and wiped the few tears that came down my face. I'm not sure what went down with her but I felt like she was telling me the truth about it not being what it seemed. I was going to make sure to see Vera and ask her what the fuck really happened. She too, had a guilty look. If I find out she had anything to do with it, baby mama or not, that's her ass.

Noah

Shit was all bad right now. Roxanne was locked up and Kasha was working my fucking nerves. I don't know why she thought we were a couple when I couldn't stand her ass. She kept popping up and bringing me food, trying to act like the perfect woman. The shit was a joke considering I knew the real Kasha. We're not going to even talk about my daughter whom she barely knew. I was losing my damn mind dealing with the women in my life, especially Roxanne's ass. She may have shot me but I still love her and I understand where she's coming from so I'm not holding it against her, shit I'm still breathing.

I went to my mom's house when I got back from the jail and she was in the kitchen on the phone with most likely my aunt Harriet, Abe's mother. The two of them were sisters and best friends. I heard her talking shit about Roxanne and my aunt must've said something about it because she sucked her teeth.

My aunt loved Roxanne, or Roxy as she called her so my mom trying to kick her back in wasn't happening. I sat down at the table with my mom still unaware of me being there. Once she turned around, she dropped the spatula and the phone, talking about I scared her. She told my aunt she'd call her back.

"Hey son. What's going on and how are my grandbabies?"

"What's going on is, I went to see Roxanne at the jail that my kids mother is in and the funniest thing happened?" She didn't say anything and took a seat next to me.

"My son tried to buck up on me."

"Whattttt?" She said not believing what I told her.

"Yea and I didn't know why until he informed me that his grandmother wished death on his mother and gave him some information we, his parents weren't ready to tell him. Care to explain?"

"It was time for him to know."

"Says who? You? Because the last I checked, me and his mother made that decision, not you. And why would you wish death on Roxanne?"

"Because she didn't tell me you were shot. I had to hear it from Kasha."

"So the fuck what?" My mom looked at me. I barely ever cursed around her but when I did, she knew I was pissed.

"She was my woman, the mother of my firstborns and you wished death on her in front of our son. And since when did you start talking to Kasha? Wait, how the fuck did she know about the shooting so fast?"

"I don't know but when Roxanne came home I didn't give her time to say anything and smacked the shit out of her."

"YOU WHAT?" I stood up mad as hell.

"Noah, she should've called me on the way and mentioned it so I could.-"

"So you could nothing. What the fuck were you thinking putting your hands on her? Did you stop and think that maybe she was going through something and wanted to make sure I was alright before she told you? Or maybe she was scared to mention it, assuming you would rush down there and get into an accident."

"I am your mother Noah."

"And she was my woman. You're sitting here talking shit about her not calling you, but your sister was down there.

112

Did she call you? Did Abe dial your number? Huh? It was other people who had your number too but I don't see you going hard at them like you are Roxanne. What's up with that?"

"I'm not talking about it anymore. I feel the way I do about the situation and its over with."

"Ok. Then why did you tell my son about Melody?" She stood up.

"I told you, I was mad she didn't tell me about you and I acted off emotions. I'm sorry."

"No you're not. Ma, I'm not sure what you and Kasha have cooking in those heads of yours but let me tell you this." She stared at me as I turned to leave.

"Roxanne is the mother of my children and will be my wife one day. Kasha was a fuck that ended up keeping a baby I didn't want. She disappeared and neglected her daughter for three years and yet; you think, I'm supposed to welcome her back with open arms. Not ever going to happen and if you don't fix shit with my girl, our mother and son relationship will cease and desist."

"Are you serious?" I opened the door.

"As a heart attack." I slammed it and went to my car and saw my lawyer left me two messages. Both of them stating he tried to get Roxanne released but she's been refusing all visitations. I thought it was only because she didn't want the kids to see her in there anymore but if she's doing the same with the lawyer, I had to make some calls and get there myself.

****

"Daddy I want candy." Melody asked as she climbed on my lap. I smiled at my other twin. All my kids resembled me and I hate she'd been isolated from her siblings. Even though I created her outside of my relationship, I didn't love her any different nor do I regret my child. All this time she had been getting the short end of the stick because I let Roxanne make me choose between her and my daughter.

"No candy but I have a surprise for you?" She smiled as she looked up at me and that shit warmed my heart. It was nothing like the relationship between a father and his kids.

"What?" she asked as her eyes got big, the same eyes my daughter Precious had.

"Remember daddy told you that you have a brother and sister?" she shook her head yes.

"Well you get to meet them today."

"Yay!" she clapped her small hands. Melody was always alone because none of the kids in my family were her age and she didn't know her siblings but today it all changed. All my kids would be under the same roof from here on out.

"Come on and let's go get you dressed and I need to find someone to do your hair. This shit is wild as hell."

"Ooh daddy said bad word." She put her hands over her mouth being extra dramatic.

"Daddy's sorry baby, now come on." After she got dressed we drove over to my aunts house because all the kids were there and she wanted to meet Melody too. I could have introduced her sooner to my aunt but knowing her she would've cursed all of us out and I didn't feel like hearing it.

"So this is supposed to be our little sister?" Precious asked with her hand on her hip as she stared at Melody. My aunt smacked her hands to put her arm down.

"Yes she is." I said putting her down to walk around.

"Well my mama only has two kids so she ain't my sister." She said rolling her eyes. I swear I don't know where the fuck these kids got this smart shit from but I was getting tired of it.

"Precious don't make me whoop yo ass!" I threatened as I gave her a look that let her know I wasn't playing. I had never whooped her but the way shit been going lately she was well on her way to a first.

"Precious she is three years old and although your daddy made a mistake, she is your sister." My aunt told her but she still wasn't trying to hear it.

"Hey Melody. I'm Noah, ya big brother."

"Hi." She smiled at lil Noah but Precious was still pouting and I knew it was because she wasn't used to sharing me. She didn't have to worry about Junior because he was a boy but I could tell she felt threatened.

"Baby girl, daddy don't love you any less, but I need you to make your sister feel welcome and not like an outsider. She's going to be living with us so I need y'all to get along."

"Does my mother know you're moving your outside child in the house?" Her ass was not having it and I knew in the long run this was going to be a problem. My aunt shook her head. I wanted to pop the fuck out of her but she's right. I was making changes quickly without thinking about how it would affect them.

"Your mom and I are no longer together and.-"

"Your fault daddy. I know you think I'm too young too understand but I do. You hurt mommy and had another baby. Now you want us all to become one family because it's out in the open. I don't have a problem with her because she's a baby but you didn't even ask us what we thought. Daddy you're selfish and how would you feel if mommy cheated on you and came back with a baby?"

"That would never happen because your mom loves me."

"Exactly daddy and I thought you loved mommy. I love you so much daddy but I hate what you did to our family. I don't want to live with you and I'm staying with my aunt until mommy comes home." She had tears running down her face as Chelsea stood there hugging her.

"She crying daddy." Melody said standing in front of me, pointing.

"Precious, I'm sorry but what's done is done."

"Yup. What's done is done and I don't have to be around you or her. My mommy said anytime I feel uncomfortable about something to remove myself." I hated how smart she was but what could I say? I fucked up and my kids weren't beat for the bullshit.

"Dad, I'll come with you but I'm with Precious. I don't want to live with you either. I know she's my sister but my mom didn't have her. Her mom doesn't like us and I know that because when Nana took us to grandmas house to get the money she had for us, she was there."

"What did she say?"

"Nothing much after I told her off."

"You know better Noah."

"Yea, well she said my mom should rot in jail and it's only a matter of time before you two get back together.

118

Grandma, well your mother, because I'm not calling her that anymore, sat there agreeing with her. Dad, we know you love us but you can't put your mistake on us." He stood up and went in the house to check on Precious.

"I don't know what to do aunty. I messed up and I thought being around all my kids was the right thing to do but mannnnn, it's stressing me the fuck out."

"Daddy. Why are you mad?" My aunt sat Melody on her lap.

"Noah, the kids are hurting, regardless of who made the decision not to tell them sooner. I see you trying to do the right thing but they're going to need time. Not only are they sharing you with another kid but their own grandmother is trying to get you and her mother back together. They don't see you fighting for their mom and they blame you for hurting and putting her in the positions she's in."

"I know but.-"

"Noah, give them time. Its still fresh and you know when Roxanne comes home she'll be able to smooth things over with them."

119

"So what am I supposed to do?"

"Continue to be there for them. For now, I would come see them without the baby and eventually ease her in their life. They miss it being the four of you. Go see Roxanne and bring her home. The kids need to know she's ok and safe before they can move on to the next thing."

"I love you aunty." She gave me a hug and kissed Melody on the cheek.

"As far as your mother goes, I've got some words for her ass and they sure aren't from the bible." We both laughed. I put Melody in her seat and went to the new condo I had for us. Only time can heal all wounds and I pray when Roxanne comes home, it does just that.

Roxanne

It was going on five months pregnant and I'm still locked up. This shit didn't get any easier and I missed my kids like crazy. I got to see them during visitation but it wasn't the same, and that wasn't even the half of it. When I found out two weeks ago I was pregnant, I also found out I will probably be here for years on attempted murder charges. I haven't told anyone about the pregnancy because I didn't know what was going to happen. Noah had gotten me a lawyer just like he said but I hadn't saw Honor or anyone else because I refused their visits.

All I wanted was my kids and I couldn't have that so fuck everyone else. I didn't mean to sound bitter but I blamed Noah for me being here. I know I pulled the trigger but had he never cheated the first time, I would have never been so insecure. Yeah, I know that sounds stupid as fuck and I'm to blame for being in here. He cheated but I could have handle that shit better than I did and now my kids are suffering because of my mistakes.

I finally saw my lawyer and he told me that even though I was being charged with assault with intent to commit murder, it's punishable by any number of years to life. When I heard the words life, I was scared shitless, I couldn't be here for the rest of my life. He claimed without Noah's testimony, all they had was hearsay, they didn't even have a weapon but these days I wasn't too sure. Especially since he was plotting against me with his mother to take my kids.

"Roxy girl don't look so down, yo ass gone be out of here soon." My Bunkie Sandra said. Sandra was cool as hell and the only female I talked to in here. She was in here for credit card fraud and had three kids in the system because of it. I was glad one of us was feeling positive because I had lost all hope the longer I stayed in here.

"Girl I don't think so, I mean I shot him a few times and almost died."

"Yeah but he ain't dead nor is he pressing charges. Even if the prosecutor picks up the case, you got a good ass lawyer and no criminal background. I don't see you spending time in jail, shit I hope you don't because one of us gotta make it up out here, shit." She laughed even though I knew she was serious as hell. This was her third time being locked up so I knew she was about to do some time.

"I hear you girl but I'm not that optimistic right now." You would be if you stop ignoring visits.

"Paul you have a visit!" the CO yelled out. I wasn't expecting a visit today so I wasn't sure who it was. I took her advice and accepted the visit but I shouldn't have.

"When I come back I need you to braid my hair in two braids please."

"I got you boo."

I got up from my bunk and waited for the CO to unlock the cell. She led me to the visiting room. I hadn't gone to court yet so I was still in the county. When I walked in the visiting room and saw Noah's mother I wanted to turn back around. All these years I thought she and I had a good relationship, when in actuality she really hated me. Now why she was here was beyond me but I was about to find out what her slick ass was up to.

"What are you doing here?" I didn't even sit down because I didn't have much to say to her ass.

"Look. I didn't come here to fight with you, and this won't take long at all. Since it looks like you'll be here for a while, the kids will be moving with Noah. I also think you should just sign over your rights. I mean it's not like you can do shit for them in prison." She replied as she rolled her eyes. I swear, I almost punched her in her shit but I kept my cool. I think God is testing me right now and I'm going to try and remain calm.

"That's not happening, you can leave and please don't bring your ass back here."

"Well, I tried to do things the right way but I'll let Noah know you refused and he'll just have to go to court like he planned to in the first place."

"What the hell are you talking about?" I asked because I was curious.

"Well since you asked, Noah was going to petition the court for custody being as though you're a danger to the kids but I told him, I'd talk to you and get you to do the right thing but it's obvious you won't, so we have no other choice but to go to court." She got up and walked away.

"You tell Noah to kiss my ass and he's not taking my kids!" I yelled at her but she never turned back around. I couldn't believe Noah was doing this. How the hell did we go from him helping me get out and forgiving me, to him taking my kids? What the hell was really going on? I headed back to my bunk feeling defeated because there was no way in hell I was going be able to compete with Noah while I was in jail. I wanted to die. I went to the door signaling the CO I was ready to go back to my cell. I didn't think shit could get any worse; my kids were my heart and to not have them, was like dying. I called Noah and told him to come up to the jail tomorrow. I needed to know what the fuck was going on.

****

"Paul, your baby daddy here and don't say you refuse the visit because his ass ain't hearing it." The guard said and walked me out to the room. His eyes almost popped out his head when he saw my stomach.

"Damn, I missed you." He hugged me and I pushed him off.

"How dare you come in here claiming you miss me, when you sent your mother up here petitioning me to take my kids?"

"First off... They are our kids. And second... I would never take them from you. If you want to know if I asked her to come up here? Yes, I did. I told her she needed to apologize for the shit she pulled." I couldn't do anything but believe him.

"Tell me exactly what she said." At first I didn't want to but the sincere look on his face made me. He was furious when I told him everything but then he went off on me.

"Why the hell have you been refusing visits from the kids?"

"Noah, I don't want them to see me like this."

"Then you should've never pulled the fucking trigger." He whispered through gritted teeth.

"Motherfucker if you never cheated on me.-" He stopped me.

"You're right. I fucked up but how many times are you going to use that as an excuse for being selfish? Huh?" I didn't say anything.

"I MESSED UP ROXANNE DAMN. EVERYONE, I CHEATED ON MY GIRL. YOU HAPPY NOW ROXANNE. EVERYONE HERE KNOWS. IS THAT WHAT YOU WANTED?"

"Noah stop it."

"Why Roxanne? The woman I'm in love with is sitting in a jail behind some stupid shit I did but I didn't put her here. She put her self here, yet blaming me."

"Noah."

"Nah. You can refuse my visits forever; I don't give a fuck but my fucking kids need to see their mother. What the fuck is wrong with you?"

"I want to see them too Noah, not like this though."

"Roxanne you could've been out of here months ago but you're so got damn selfish you refused the lawyers visits." I put my head down.

"Yea he told me. You are one selfish bitch and when you get out of here, maybe it is best that we never be together again. I've done all I can to show you how sorry I was but in your eyes it didn't matter because all you saw was what I did. You never forgave me Roxanne did you?" I refused to answer.

"Dammit Roxanne. I lost out on three years with my daughter over you."

"Oh so you would take me back if I cheated and got pregnant?"

"Probably not but I wouldn't have kept you around to keep you from being happy with someone else. I can't even be mad at you because I let it happen." He scoffed up a laugh with his hands on the top of his head.

"This is what's going to happen." He sat in front of me.

"You are going to be released in the morning. Your mom will be here to pick you up and take you to the house I have waiting for you. The kids are expecting you and I swear on everything you better fucking tell them it was your choice not to see them and it wasn't something I did. We're going to go down to the courthouse the following day and get joint custody of the kids and you're going to file for child support. When the baby is born I'll be there. After that I'm fucking done with you. The only time you should ring my phone is if something is wrong with my kids and even then you don't have to because they have a phone. If by some chance you see me out and about don't say two fucking words to me. Are we clear?"

"Noah don't do this." I stood up grabbing his arm.

"You did this Roxanne. You can blame me for the cheating and a baby but everything else you did. I'm giving you your freedom, now stay the fuck away from me." He snatched away and stormed out the room.

What have I done?

Honor

The day I called Abe up to the hospital to tell him about the baby and what happened with his ex's brother, I found out he was sleeping around. I should have expected it but when a nigga is in your ear telling you everything you want to hear, you try not to think about him doing you wrong. I cried for days after he left and it was so bad they almost admitted me to the crazy floor because I kept talking to myself. I tried to figure out, how I didn't see it.

They released me a week later. The sores were gone but they still had me taking medication as a precaution. The surgery was a success and I can still have kids in the future, which won't be for a while.

The day I came home, my house was spotless and there were roses all over. I had bags of clothes, jewelry, purses and shoes in my bedroom. I was so mad, I gathered it all up and took it to his mom house and asked her to tell him not to do it again. She knew he cheated on me because I told her when I let her know about the pregnancy. Of course, she let him have it and told me he kept saying he was sorry but was he really?

I packed all my things up and moved into a smaller apartment across town. This little insurance job paid decent but not enough to live where I was. It felt good moving though because there were no memories here, and Abe didn't know where I was.

"How are you sweetie?" I asked Roxanne who had been home a few months and gave birth two weeks ago to another boy. She came home and had the baby early but because his lungs were clear and since he was almost six pounds she was able to bring him home. Noah seemed ecstatic but with everything they had going on, he refused to be around her.

"I'm good. Trying to keep it together." She closed the door and walked in the bedroom. I picked her up to go have a few drinks. Her mom moved in with her, and she was happy I was getting her out the house.

The kids were in the living room watching a movie. We left ten minutes later and found some hole in the wall. We sat at the bar and watched as some people did karaoke. Drunk people and Karaoke can be quite the combination.

"Listen Roxanne. We haven't really spoken about what all happened but I want you to know that I'm here for you."

"Thanks sis. I thought about what you and Noah said and a lot of what happened is my fault. I was selfish and only thinking of myself when I had two kids and a man to consider." I didn't say a word because she was right.

"Don't look now but Abe just got here and he's with some woman."

"Its ok Roxy. I'm over it now and besides its most likely the woman he's been sleeping with.

He and the woman sat at a table for two while Roxy and I stayed at the bar having drink after drink. It felt good to be out and we had a lot of fun. She even got on stage and did I will survive by Gloria Gaynor. I couldn't stop laughing and made sure to record her ass. She was a little drunk and it would be funny to see her face when she hears how bad she sounds tomorrow. I thought about going up there to do I ain't fucking with you, but I didn't know all the words.

"What are you doing here Roxanne?" I heard Noah behind me. When I looked, his face was turned up.

"I thought you said not to say two fucking words to you if I saw you out." She rolled her eyes and tossed back another shot.

"Yo, are you drunk?" He asked as she tossed back another lemon drop.

"Why does it matter? We co-parent, I get child support and you are living your life with the daughter I made you miss time out on. Come on Honor, this nigga is blowing my high." She tried to get up and almost fell.

"Take your ass the fuck home." He said standing in front of her.

"I'll go home when I feel like it. Matter of fact, my new man is waiting on me to come over." She grabbed her purse and before I could say anything, Noah had her back bent over the bar with his hand around her throat. I was punching him in his arm telling him to get off.

"Roxanne, I swear to God if you are fucking someone else."

"Get the fuck off me Noah." She pushed him and he removed his hand from her throat but stood in front of her.

"You told me it was over and to never speak to you again. You hear I'm messing with someone else and you want to choke me. How does it feel to even think I'd lay with another man? Huh? Every time you left the house all I saw was you in bed with another woman. Do you know how that feels? I've lost many nights of sleep and cried plenty of times over you but no more." He moved and she stood up crying.

"You say I'm selfish. You damn right. I was selfish when it came to my family and I always will be. Not only did you make me share you with another woman, you made our kids share you with another kid who didn't come from me. I was selfish when it came to my pussy too Noah, something you couldn't do with your dick. If you didn't hate me before you'll hate me now. I'm going to find me someone to love and respect me and when I do he's going to get all my love. The way I used to have you moaning, he's going to get it even better. Fuck you nigga." She tried to walk away and he snatched her back by the hair.

"Come on man. Why you putting hands on her?" Some dude came up out of nowhere asking. Abe fucked him up and then it was an all out brawl in there. I was walking Roxanne out when some chick stopped us outside.

"Are you Honor?"

"Why?"

"Because I'm Monica. I wanted to say thanks for leaving Abe alone. Now that you're no longer in the picture he gives me his full attention. Oh, I'm sorry about the baby."

"What did you say?"

"Let it go Honor."

"What? He was upset about the baby and told me."

"Yo Monica. What the fuck you doing?" Abe came out where we were. I punched him hard as hell in the face. He grabbed both of my wrists and threw me against the wall.

"Get the fuck off me."

"What's wrong?"

"What's wrong is, I tell you how we lose a baby and you run to the bitch you're fucking and tell her. What the hell is wrong with you?"

"I didn't tell her shit."

"Abe, you're the only one I told. Hell Roxanne didn't know until she came home." He let me go and yanked her up by the hair.

"Who the fuck told you about my girl losing our baby."

"I'm not your girl."

"Honor you will always be mine." Monica sucked her teeth.

"Ok. My sister works in dietary at the hospital and she was there handed out lunches when you were in the room." I remember a chick putting my lunch on the tray table but I didn't pay her any mind.

"Abe, stay away from me, and Monica, I don't care what you do with him, don't ever feel its ok to approach me over him."

"Honor."

"No Abe. Its over between us. Why can't you get that through your head? You hurt me too many times to forgive and I just want to be happy."

"Well he'll be happy in six months because I'm having his baby." Abe snapped his neck to look at her. I tried not to cry because I did tell him we were over but damn he got another woman pregnant right after we lost ours. Was he trying to replace the baby?

"I was going to tell you tonight when we got home."

"Home. You live together."

"Yup. He brought a condo and I'm there everyday. I still have my own place but you can say it's my place too. Here's my key." She dangled it in my face. It was as if the color drained from his face as she revealed all this information.

"That's great. Have a good life Abe." I wiped my face and walked off, only to be lifted off the ground.

"Get off of me." He continued walking to my car where Roxanne was able to make it to, drunk and all.

"Honor, please let me talk to you."

"No. Absolutely not."

"Stop acting childish."

"I'm not childish Abe. I'm taking care of me from now on. I knew you moved on from the hickeys and seeing your photos on Instagram. I knew. I didn't know you made her your woman, moved her in and planned a family with her though. Are you trying to replace the child we lost?"

"How could you ask me that?"

"Ugh, because she's pregnant and you live together."

"I don't think she's pregnant because I always strap up. I think she told you that to get you mad."

"Do you live with her?"

"I don't but she does have a key. If you want me back, I'll snatch it from her right now."

"Nope. She can keep it. I will never want you again. Good luck with everything." He hugged me and I broke down in his arms. I have been through so much and it seemed like the walls were closing in on me.

"How much longer are you going to be? I'm horny." I heard and Abe blacked out on her and told her to go wait in the car.

"I love you and only you Honor." He lifted my chin.

"Are you ok to drive?"

"I'm fine. Go tend to your woman. I'm sorry for crying all over you."

"Don't apologize." I looked up and his eyes were glassy.

"I will always love you Abe, you know that but you moved on and its time I do the same. Goodbye." I left him standing there and this time he didn't run after me. I got to Roxanne's house and decided to crash there on the couch. Unfortunately, Noah came to the house and I had to sit out there for two hours listening to him vent about Roxanne.

I was tired and happy as hell when he called it a night, only thing is, he went upstairs. I know he wanted her back and the feeling was mutual but until they talked like adults nothing would ever be right between them. I picked up my phone and saw Abe sent me ten messages asking where I was; if he could come see me and in one he asked could he make love to me one last time. He was delirious if he thought that. I shut my phone off and once my head hit the pillow I was out.

Noah

I was talking to Kasha's dumb ass on the phone when Abe called to tell me Roxanne was at the bar. I hung up, threw my clothes on and rushed over there. Don't ask me why, when I specifically told her not to say two words to me if she saw me on the street. But here I go rushing to get her. Luckily, my aunt had Melody; otherwise my ass would've been stuck.

All the shit went down at the bar and I heard Roxy loud and clear as she told me how selfish she was with her family and I should've been the same. I'm not the one to go for all this arguing and shit. I took my ass in the house after sitting and talking to Honor for almost two damn hours. I walked up the steps and could hear faint noises. I opened the door and Roxy was on the bed, balled up crying.

I took her clothes off and carried her in the bathroom to shower. I could see vomit all over the bed and floor. She could never hold her liquor. I changed the sheets while she washed up and used some towels to clean the rest up. I heard her shut the water off and went back in to hand her a towel. Her eyes were red and her breath was horrendous. She stepped out and stood in front of the sink preparing to brush her teeth after gargling with the mouthwash. Neither of us said two words as she finished getting herself together.

"I'm sorry for making you miss out on Melody." She said getting in the bed.

"I took my anger out on her and it wasn't right. You love your kids and me putting you in a predicament to choose, is fucked up. I was scared you'd sleep with her mom again. I figured it wouldn't happen if you weren't there. I couldn't take losing you to her again." I stared at her as she spoke the truth; finally. I never understood why she made me choose and now I see.

"I love you Noah and I hope you forgive me. I will try my hardest to get the kids on the same page. Melody should be able to know them." Still not knowing what to say, my eyes were locked on hers.

"Noah, are you listening?" I cleared my throat.

"Yes and I'm sorry for cheating. To be honest, I'm not sure why I did it. I never wanted kids outside of you and when

141

she told me she was pregnant, believe when I say, I begged her to terminate it. Unfortunately, when she told me it was too late and now Melody is here." She got out the bed and came to me by the dresser. Her hands ran under my shirt and I could feel myself becoming aroused.

"Roxanne." I bit down on my bottom lip when she took her shirt off.

"Noah do you still love me?"

"That's one question you never have to ask." Her hands were at my jeans.

"This isn't why I'm here Roxy and it's not going to solve anything. Dammit." I moaned out after feeling her tongue glide over the tip.

"It doesn't, but you are the only man who is allowed to touch me." She was sucking and jerking me off.

"Damn right. That ain't never going to change."

"Then I want some of this." I stood her up and my dick was mad as hell. She had my nut at the top ready to shoot out.

"Roxanne, I love the fuck out of you but I can't do this." She stepped away and put her shirt back on.

"Lock the door on your way out."

"Roxanne, I want you real bad but you're going to regret it in the morning. Right now, you're horny from the liquor and we both know I'm going to end up getting you pregnant again; on purpose." She looked at me and I shrugged my shoulders because I meant it.

"If you want this or me, it has to be because we're in a relationship and not a baby mama and baby daddy having sex, just because. I don't want that with us. I want my family back and if it's not something you can do, then I can't be with you."

"I want my family too, but.-"

"Melody right."

"No. Her mama, your mama and.-"

"Roxy, I'm no worried about them and you shouldn't either. They have no influence whatsoever on what I do with you. None!" I stated with confidence.

"Noah you and the kids are my life." I took her face in my hands.

"Mine too." She stared up at me.

"Do you know how it feels when all you have just dies.

I've tried and tried to deny that I need you but still you remain on my mind. I want my family too but.-"

"But nothing Roxy. If you can accept Melody, nothing else matters. I need you just as much as you need me." She nodded her head but remained quiet. I put my forehead on hers and let my lips touch hers.

"I love you Roxanne."

"I love you too Noah. Bring Melody here tomorrow. It's Sunday, so we'll be here all day. Maybe we can get the kids to meet properly and not the way you did it."

"Are you sure?"

"You don't want me to meet her?"

"I'm not going to answer you. Goodnight." I went to walk out and she grabbed my arm.

"Let me at least finish what I started." I didn't even bother to stop her this time. It's been a minute since I had sex and if this is what she wanted, then she got it.

"I missed this. Suck it all out baby." I slowly pumped in and out and enjoyed her allowing me to coat her throat.

"Goodnight baby." She pecked my lips and went to get

in bed. Her ass was showing as she crawled to the top. I don't even care if it was on purpose.

"Oh hell no." I could hear her laugh. I made sure the door was locked, took all my clothes off and climbed on top of her.

"I thought you said.-" she laughed and wrapped her arms around my neck.

"You play too much." We ended up sexing one another a few times before falling asleep. This is my family and no one is about to take them from me.

****

I woke up and Roxy wasn't in the bed. My phone said it was after ten and it shocked me because I can't sleep past six, ever. I went in the bathroom and grabbed a toothbrush from under the counter. She was big on having extra everything in the house. I brushed my teeth, washed my face and went downstairs to leave.

I text my aunt and asked her to get Melody ready so I could bring her over. This is going to be a challenge but if Roxy is down for it, we may as well get it out the way.

"Daddy, what are you doing here?" I heard my son ask and my daughter turned around and rolled her eyes.

"Remember her age baby." Roxy said as I made my way to her. I snatched her ass up off the couch and made her look at me.

"Precious, you can be mad all you want but the one thing you won't do is ever feel it's ok to disrespect me. I know this situation is hard but I am your father." She had tears coming down her eyes. I never yell or raise my voice at her and I could see it bothering her.

"I'm sorry. I just want you and mommy back together and we be a family like we used to be."

"Precious, I can see that what your mom and I go through has an affect on you. However, we would never neglect any of you because of it. I call you every morning; I drop off money or anything you need because you don't want to be around me. You don't see me acting the way you do."

"You're a grown up and mommy said adults can't get mad at kids." I looked up and Roxy was standing there smiling.

"Your mom is right and it's exactly why I would never

146

take my anger out on my kids. However, it doesn't mean you can say or do what you want to adults either. Always give out the same respect you want given back to you." Precious nodded her head and Roxanne asked both of them to come in the kitchen. She gestured for me to follow and handed me a plate of food. They sat down and waited for her to speak. Hell yea, I'm letting her handle it. The last time I tried, it didn't go so well.

"Precious and Junior, today your dad is bringing Melody over." I saw both of their eyes pop open.

"I don't want you mad at daddy or her because of me."

"But she's not your daughter mommy." Precious said pissing me off. We all know she's not by Roxanne and she keeps bringing it up.

"I know but she's daddy's and your sister. Its time to move past it and get back to being the family we were."

"Dad, are you and mom back together?" I looked at her and she nodded yes.

"Your mom said yes, so I guess we are."

"Well, can I come with you today?"

"Junior, you could come with me any day. Your mom doesn't have to be my woman for that to happen."

"I know but I didn't want mommy to be angry because I would be around Melody." I gave Roxanne a hard stare. This is the reason I told her we should've told them sooner.

"Junior, I'm sorry if I ever made you and Precious feel like you had to be mad at daddy because I was. It was never my intention." He gave her a hug and I finished eating and took Precious in the other room with me. I sat her on the chair and kneeled down in front of her.

"You will always be my first daughter and no one, will ever take my love from you." She wiped her tears. I knew it was why she stayed angry with me.

"But daddy she's a girl too and.-"

"You will always be my first daughter Precious. No one will ever take your place in my heart. Plus, what happens if your mom has another baby and she's a girl? Are you going to be angry with her too?"

"I would have if you didn't tell me not too worry. Can you only give mommy boys from now on?" I laughed and lifted her up. She may be a big girl but she is always going to be my baby girl. I kissed her cheek and told her I'd be back later. Roxanne came behind me with and had her arms on my waist.

"I'm happy you're home Noah."

"Are you?" I kissed her and heard Precious say yuk and walk away.

"I am. I want you to know I'm on birth control right now, so there's no boy or girl in my stomach. I'm telling you because I don't want you to wonder why I'm not getting pregnant or that I've had an abortion. I would never terminate another baby and when Lil man gets to be at least one we can have another one."

"I'm holding you to that. I want six of my kids running around."

"Six?"

"Yup. You know I want a big family and you're it for me so you have to give me what I want."

"I don't know about six but you can definitely get whatever you want from me." She said and put her index finger in her mouth.

"Stop playing. Let me go get Melody and I promise to handle the shit out of your body later."

"You better." I pecked her lips and walked out he door looking up to God and thanking him for answering my prayers. It took him a while but they always say he'll come when you need him the most and he did.

I started cleaning the house after Noah left to pick
Melody up. I knew the only way we could get back to where
we were, is if I accepted her and right now to have my man
back, I'd do anything. I'm not weak by all means but like
Honor said, "*If I forgave him then I need to accept the baby.*"
I'm fine with doing so; it's the mama and his mom who has me
on the nervous side.

His mom flipped on me out of nowhere and she say its
over the abortions and it very well may be. She is heavily into
church, (even though sometimes she doesn't act like it) and on
many of occasions voiced her opinion on pro life and pro
choice. I never paid her any mind and had no idea her or Noah
were aware of the two I had. I hated her ever since the day she
dropped the bomb about my kids having another sibling. It
wasn't her choice and I'm going to make sure she knows it.

Two hours later I had the house spotless the way I
wanted and was sitting on the couch feeding lil man. My mom
had been a great help and I appreciated her for coming to stay
with me. She told me this morning; now that Noah is back she

would go home. I begged her to stay and she walked out the room laughing and said her man needed her. I could have thrown up hearing her say those words. I'm not saying she doesn't deserve love and I see why my own kids act the way they do when Noah and I kiss.

Precious came and sat next to me with her Ipad. She may be a daddy's girl but her ass stays up under me just as much. The door opened a few minutes later and I heard some feet running in the living room where we were. A commercial was on for some Paw Patrol shit and Melody must've heard it because she made it in here before it went off.

I saw her turn around, stare at me and Precious and run over to Junior. She held his hand and hid behind his leg as if we couldn't see her. Noah laughed and Junior told her to let his leg go because she was squeezing it too tight but she held on. I handed my son to Noah and went to where she stood. I kneeled down and introduced myself and she let me shake her hand.

"You don't have to be scared over here Melody."

"She's mean." She pointed to Precious who had a devilish grin on her face.

"She's not mean Melody. She doesn't know you and that's why you're here. I may not be your mommy, but these are your brothers and sisters."

"Baby."

"Yes he's a baby. That's your brother Trevon but we call him lil man. Do you want to hold him?" she nodded her head yes and Noah sat her next to him and held his head while she did.

Noah kept Melody over all day and eventually she made herself at home. She ran around the house most of the time and didn't even bother to take a nap. Precious asked if she could sleep over and at first I wasn't sure but she begged me. Somehow throughout the day, they became best sisters, I guess. I let her give Melody a bath with me supervising and got her ready for bed. Unfortunately, Melody wanted to stay in the room with us.

"Why are you staring at me?" I asked Noah once he came in the room after locking up the house.

"Because I think she's found her mom."

"Noah!"

"I'm serious Roxy. She has been around everyone lately but you're the only one she wants to lie under. Hell, my mom and hers tried to get her to sleep and she gives them a hard time. You say its time for bed and *BAM*, she has no problem."

"I'm not trying to take her mother's spot."

"What mother? She doesn't call anyone mommy and Kasha's stupid ass only comes by to visit if I'm there. My mother told me she'll call and ask for me and when she tells her I'm not there, she thinks of a reason to hang up. My mother said its because she's in a rush to do something." I gave him the side eye.

"Exactly Roxanne." He laid in the bed and tried to move Melody, who opened her eyes and snuggled back under me. I had to chuckle a little because it was funny.

"I know this is awkward but thank you for accepting her." I shushed him with my fingers.

"I love you and she's a part of you, so I love her too. Noah, if you ever cheat.-"

"Never gonna happen. I didn't after you found me in

the hotel."

"Good."

"You know I still haven't figured out who came for me at Paul's house or how I got upstairs."

"You'll figure it out and when you do, kill him or them." He looked at me grinning.

"You already know baby."

"You know we can't have sex tonight."

"Hell if we can't" He tried to move Melody and she grabbed on to my clothes tighter and started whining.

"Roxanne you better take her in the other room. I missed out on this long enough and last night was just a taste."

"You are a brat."

"And. Go on now. I'm about to take a shower and come out butt naked with a hard dick. You need to be ready." I started laughing hard as hell and almost woke her up. I took her in the other room with Precious and put her in the bed with her closer to the wall. I closed the door and went in my room. The shower was still going so I went in the bathroom.

"No need to wait for you to get out when I'm right

here." He turned around and smiled.

"Then assumed the position. You know I haven't been in that ass in a while."

"What are you waiting for?" I'm not even going to explain all the nasty shit we did. Just know our night was perfect.

****

It's been a few days and I've been meaning to stop by his moms to give her a piece of my mind. I dropped my son off at my mothers and the other kids were in school. Melody was put in a different school because Noah didn't want anyone trying to take her. It took us two days to pick one out. It was my fault though because I wanted her in a good one with cameras. We all know that preschool workers been doing foul shit to kids lately.

I pulled up on his mom's street and saw her on the porch talking to his stupid baby mother Kasha. I swear this woman is fake as hell. One minute she grinning in my face and the next she hates me and does it with the other baby mama. *Shady ass bitch*. I walked up to them and their conversation could be heard, as loud as they were. His mom mentioned my name and said Noah would be devastated and she can't have that. I tried to hear more but they noticed me. I gave a fake wave and smile.

"Can I help you?" Kasha asked with her hands on her hips.

"Not at all. This house doesn't belong to you; therefore, you can't help me with a damn thing. You however, have some explaining to do about the shit you came to the jail talking."

"I already told my son.-"

"I know he told me. Telling him you didn't say what I told him, as if I need to lie." She waved me off and told Kasha she'd see her later.

"Oh Kasha wait!"

"What made you come back after all these years? And please don't say Noah because as all three of us know." I pointed.

"He's my man, my baby daddy and soon to be husband."

"Husband. My son isn't marrying you."

157

"Oh you think he's going to marry this deadbeat baby momma of his? Think again sweetie. He may have cheated but he sacrificed everything for his family and fought to get us back, twice I may add. I know you don't think highly of me and I'm not sure why but I can tell you this." I stood closer to them.

"If any of you even think about touching my family, Noah will be the last person you should be afraid of."

"My daughter isn't your family." I started walking away. This situation is about to get real ugly.

"She'll be calling me mommy soon, since her real one hasn't ever been around and only wants to see her if Noah's there."

"BITCH." She yelled out and came running behind me.

"I wish the fuck you would put your hands on her." I saw Noah coming up behind me with Abe.

"Babe, I didn't know you were coming." He kissed my lips and grabbed my hand.

"Once you text me you were on your way, I knew it wouldn't go the way you wanted. You tried babe and that's all you can do. I don't want you over here again trying to make peace."

"Fuck her Noah. She's saying my baby will be calling her mommy and.-"

"And what? She will soon enough." She was mad as hell he said that.

"Melody has no idea who you are and when you are around her, she stays under me. Get your childish ass out of here."

"Oh babe, when I walked up, her and your mom we're discussing me. I'm not sure about what, but I heard my name and how devastated you would be if it happened." He turned to look at me and I shrugged my shoulders. I didn't have any more information because they stopped when they saw me. He grabbed Kasha by her hair and literally dragged her to the front door. His mom came out and he dropped her on the porch.

"Whatever you got cooked up with this bitch stops now. If anything happens to Roxanne or my kids, I promise you, I will not hesitate to kill you."

"You would kill your own mother Noah."

"Nah, I'd have you moved far away from me but her, I'll kill her on sight. Fuck with it if you want." He lifted me on his shoulders and the three of us went to the car.

"Go home and get my pussy ready. They pissed me off and I need to relieve this anger and stress."

"Don't threaten me with good dick. Be home in twenty or you ain't getting shit."

"Yea ok." He smacked my ass and waited for me to pull off. I was going to find out what his baby mom and mother was up to, if it's the last thing I do.

Abe

"What you think about the shit Roxanne said?" I asked Noah as we sat outside his house.

"I'm not taking the threat likely if that's what you're asking me. Kasha returned for a reason and it damn sure ain't Melody."

"My man said he saw her with Duke and his people at the club the last few weekends."

"Oh yea. I'm about to put someone on it." We slapped hands and he got out the car.

I drove over to my moms' house thinking of what would be a reason for Kasha to come for Roxanne. Lately it seemed as if Noah was a target and we had no idea why. He is very low key, we don't dabble in the drug game any longer and everything we have is legit. It's definitely some shady shit going down. I got to my moms house and walked inside.

I could hear my mom talking so imagine my surprise to see Honor in there with Chelsea sitting next to her. I looked her over and she is still beautiful as ever. Nothing about her changed, except she gained a few pounds. I walked over and lifted her out the seat to get a hug.

"You smell good." I let her go and hugged Chelsea and then my mom.

"Hello to you too." I see nothing's changed." She pointed to my neck.

"The least you could do is tell her to put them lower. You may have a lot of tattoos but they're still showing." She rolled her eyes and told my mom and daughter she would speak to them later.

"Let me talk to you real quick Honor." I caught her at the door.

"What's up Abe?" She kept walking. I grabbed her arm to get her to stop.

"Why you crying?"

"No reason."

"Stop lying and tell me."

"I've been emotional since the baby and your mom is the only one I talk to about it because Roxanne is busy with the kids." She wiped her face with the sleeve of her shirt.

"You can call me. It was my baby too."

"Yea but I was only a few months and I didn't want you to ask why was I so upset."

"I would never say that. I know of women who had a tubal pregnancy at four weeks and it hit them hard. Don't assume you'll know what I'll say, just ask. Honor, you are the only woman besides those two in there who will get me to drop any and everything to come to you."

"Why couldn't you stop slinging dick and wait for me?" I had to look at her to see if she was serious. When I noticed she was, I leaned her against the car and stood in front of her.

"Let me hit you with some real shit right now so this question never comes up again." She folded her arms and stood there.

"Baby girl, I'm thirty one years old and I just did eleven fucking years behind bars." She gave me a, *that's your fault* look.

"Yea, it was my fault and I'm not debating that. However, eleven years is a long time with no freedom and no pussy. I came home and started messing with this chick Monica, who you met and the more you pushed me away, the

163

closer I got to her."

"But I didn't Abe. I wanted you but I wasn't ready."

"You had eleven years to get ready for me. Eleven Honor. When you let me make love to you, I stopped messing with her and that's the Gods honest truth. I blocked her and made sure not to go anywhere she'd be. But when you told me you weren't ready for a relationship and all the other shit you said, I kept it moving. Honor, you want me to wait but you don't even know when you'll be ready." She didn't say anything.

"I love the hell out of you but I'm too old to be waiting for you to decide what you want. If you thought for one second I would be without pussy after all the years wasted, you were mistaken. I wanted you as my woman and eventually my wife but you have a lot going on in that pretty little head of yours. When you get it together and if I'm available, it's me and you all day."

"I want you now Abe." I had to laugh.

"You only want me so she can't, and I don't want you like that. She is my woman now Honor and I'm trying to be a better man by not cheating on her. I didn't do it to you when we started messing around and I'm not about to do it with her."

"Fuck it." She swung the car door open.

"You're right. It's time to move on. We're not good together and we know it. Shit, two times trying and it still hasn't worked. Yea, I'd see no use in trying anymore." She sat in her car and slammed the door.

"Honor."

"Nah. It's ok Abe. You spit some real shit and I respect it. Enjoy your day and life. It's time I do the same." She sped off and almost ran into a car. How the hell she mad at me because she don't know what she wants?

＊＊＊＊＊＊＊＊＊＊＊＊＊＊＊

I tried to call Honor that night and days and weeks after. She changed her number and asked Roxanne not to give it to me. I didn't know what to do at this point. I'm cool with what Monica and I have going on but there's no love here. She could drop dead tomorrow and I'll be ok.

It may sound harsh, however, she isn't someone I see myself with in the long run. To be honest she is a good woman and can sex the hell out of a man but she isn't for me. My heart is with someone else.

I love and I'm in love with Honor but I can't sit around waiting. Some may say if I feel this way why don't I fight for her. You can't fight for someone who doesn't know what they want. I shitted on her when we were young and I regret it each time I think about it. I come home to see she's still around and has feelings for me; yet, she's still closed off. A nigga is only going to wait around for so long. I'm not forcing any chick to be in my life; either she wants to be in it or she doesn't.

"Abe can you help me out with this zipper?" Monica asked as I waited for her to get dressed. We were going to some dinner her parents were having. She asked me to pick her up around seven thirty and here it is eight o clock and she still isn't ready.

Oh yea, I snatched my keys from her the night she told Honor about staying with me. I had given her one because she'd be waiting in my bed at night when I came home. She blew it though, because I don't play those childish ass games.

"You look nice." I zipped up the red dress that had a

166

split up the side. Her shoes and accessories matched perfect too.

"Thanks babe. You look mighty handsome yourself. I can't wait to get you home." I smiled when she used one of my lines.

"We don't have to go." I didn't care to be around her stuck up ass parents. They took one look at me and made their assumptions of who I was.

"Lets go before you change your mind." She grabbed my hand and led me out the door. Monica knew it was a matter of time and I would definitely say forget it.

We parked behind one of the cars where we wouldn't be blocked in. I know if her parents are bougie, their friends are most likely the same. The atmosphere when we stepped in wasn't as bad as I thought. There were quite a few younger cats in here from off the streets. It made me wonder what type of dinner this really is. One dude who caught my eye was Duke and on his arm was Kasha.

Duke is an up and coming street pharmacist who paid his dues as a corner boy from what I hear on the streets. He did a bid for a few years, so I guess he had that under his belt. Unfortunately, his sudden rise to power has made him greedy; therefore, he has a lot of snakes on his team getting ready for a takedown. Don't get me wrong, I'm sure he knows but any real leader would've taken them out by now.

I had to laugh at how stupid Kasha looked as he admired some woman with his boy, Grady. From behind she had a nice ass body, her hair was long and she had some fuck me heels on. She turned around and shock was written all over my face. Honor locked eyes with mine, grabbed Grady's hand and left the room. Monica had a smirk on her face as if she knew Honor would be here. I didn't say a word for the rest of the night. I watched Monica mingle with the crowd and caught her speaking with Duke in private a few times.

"Hello Abe." I turned around and Honor stood there smiling. I gave her a hug and didn't want to let go. Monica coming in my direction made me.

"How are you? I've been trying to call you."

"I needed some time alone to get my mind right."

"Hello. Honor, is it?" Monica asked and Honor gave

her a fake smile.

"Yes it is, but you know that. It's good to see you Abe. Take care." She kissed my cheek and went to leave.

"I'm taking very good care of him. Don't worry your pretty head about that. What you can do is worry about Grady?" She turned to look and he had two chicks around him. Honor shrugged her shoulders and took a sip of his drink.

"He's looking for someone to fuck tonight." We both looked at her.

"Yea Grady and I work together now and he asked me to come because he didn't want to come alone. We even drove in separate cars so he can take her home. Isn't that your sister Monica?" Honor was being smart but I liked it and had a smirk on my face.

"You have Abe now but when I want him back, they'll be nothing or no one to stop me."

"Excuse me. He doesn't want you."

"Even you don't believe what you're saying. Have a good night Abe." I grabbed her hand and pulled her into me.

"I'm not waiting forever." I whispered in her ear and

she smiled.

"I promise you, it won't be." This time she kissed my lips. I was getting ready to slide my tongue in but Monica was tugging on my shirt.

"Told you." Honor walked away. I watched as she sashayed over to Grady. They spoke briefly and she left. Damn! Why couldn't she ask me to come tonight?

"If you want her go ahead."

"Fuck outta here. You heard what she said. She ain't ready so enjoy your time with me because when she is, I'm out." She sucked her teeth and stormed away from me. I saw her parents staring at me and gave both of them the finger. Her mom pretended to clutch her pearls with her dramatic ass. This is the exact reason I don't do these types of parties.

"What's your name?" Some chick asked.

"Fuck you and leave you is my name and yours." Her smile faded and she hauled ass. I told Monica I'd see her later. This isn't my type of party and I damn sure ain't staying.

Duke

"Fuck me harder Duke. Shit baby. I'm cumming again." Monica yelled out. I had her bent over the sink in the upstairs bathroom while her so called man was downstairs.

"I'm cumming inside and I swear you better not get rid of my baby again."

"Duke, I can't have a baby with you and I'm with him. Ohhhhhh fuckkkkk." Her juices were all over my legs.

"In a few months he'll be gone anyway so it won't matter. I'm putting my son in you." I filled her up and stood there watching her try to catch her breath.

"I love you baby." I kissed up her spine and helped her up. I reached under the sink and grabbed a washcloth to clean us both up.

"I love you too and why are you still with the cokehead? I thought you were leaving her alone since she couldn't get close to Noah." She was talking about Kasha who had come to me to help get her baby daddy back.

I met her in a club and only made plans to fuck her until she mentioned who her baby daddy was. I kept her around and regretted it. It was ridiculous how much she loved Noah, who had her as a sidepiece and she popped up pregnant.

"I was until she told me he had something big coming up."

"Something like what?"

"Him and Abe have been speaking with the connect and the only time you do that is when you're getting back in the game. I'm going to make sure it doesn't happen."

"He hasn't said anything around me. I do want the bitch Honor to suffer a slow death though. As long as she's around he won't get close to me. I swear she does shit to spite me."

"Don't let her. Damn, I want to make love to you. Let's go in one of the rooms."

"Baby I have to show my face. Come on. He's going away next weekend so I'm all yours and I promise to let you have your way with me." I kissed the back of her neck and squeezed her ass on the way out. She went one way and I went the other.

I walked in the dining area and could see Grady hanging all over other chicks. I swear he was about to make us lose everything. Ever since he hooked up with Honor and she let him go down on her, he's been acting strange. Yea, he's had tons of women but this nigga seems to be stuck on her and haven't even fucked her yet. I saw the way Abe made sure to keep his eye on her and a few minutes after they spoke, she bounced.

"What the fuck yo? You over here causing a scene."

"Man this bitch mad because I asked the other one to join us." He was talking about Monica's sister. They've been sleeping together for a minute now and she's acting like a damn stalker.

"Ok but if you're supposed to be with Honor, you can't be out here playing single. We have to keep her as close as possible."

Grady had to get a job to keep his parole office off his back. Fortunately for him, we knew the dude Honor worked for. He gave him a job and she was the one training him. He started taking her out. She left and he's fucking up to get more pussy. I wanted as many people close to Abe as possible, so when the time came to take him out, we'd have enough ammunition. As far as I can see, Honor is just what we need.

"I'm ready to cut her off, for real yo."

"It's that serious?"

"Nah. The thing is, I'm feeling Honor and she is definitely wife material but she's holding back. All she allowed me to do is eat her pussy, which hey, I'm not complaining because her pussy taste good as hell. Shorty ain't over him and it makes it harder for me to fuck her. And we all know once she gets the dick, there is no Abe." Grady is a cocky ass nigga and I blame the chicks who stalk him for it.

"Look. Go after her and make it seem as if you're trying to make it right. Show her you didn't leave with anyone else."

"This my last time bro and if she doesn't give up the ass, I'm out or I will make her disappear. Got me working extra hard to get it." He started popping shit on his way out. I knew he wouldn't harm her because as he stated, she is wife material. He's mad she won't allow him to walk all over her or chase him.

I went in the other room and saw Kasha nodding the hell off. Morgan came over and asked me to get her out of

174

there. The party is for the men to invest in my up and coming project, which is building a new shopping mall. I may not be rich but with my drug empire and these people investing their money, I'll have millions in no time. Most of them I met already and being Monica's family loved me; they decided to invite some of their friends as well.

Monica and I used to date off and on for years. We were in love and on our way to marriage, however, I went to jail for five years and she moved on. I came home, built my empire and got a name in the streets as the man who is the shit. Her parents think I come from a rich family and we're going to keep it that way. If they knew who I was, they would've never thrown this party or allowed Monica to be with me.

She told her parents Abe was a friend from her job. They were under the assumption we were still together. Long story short, I'm about to take all his money I know he has locked away. Kasha is the only one who is close with Noah and he's giving her a hard time so it's taking a little longer than I expected.

"Lets go." I snatched her up and she almost toppled

over some old white lady.

"Whattttt?" She whined pissing me off more.

"I'm taking you home." We were at my car when I heard Monica yell to call her later.

"Oh now that you finished fucking her, we can leave now?" I snapped my neck to look at her.

"What? You think I didn't see you two come out of different directions but at the same time. You claimed you loved me. How is it possible when you're fucking her?" I started my car and pulled off.

"I do love you Kasha but this getting high shit ain't working." I had to tell her something.   I couldn't stand her and the pussy is trash. I needed her to get inside but unfortunately, it's not working and I'm going to have to go with plan b, which is take both of their bitches and hold them for ransom. This waiting is becoming too much and I can see myself getting locked up, messing with her.

Honor

"What Grady?" I opened the door when he showed up at my house. Grady is sexy as hell to me and his tongue game is great but he's just something to do right now. I know he's out there doing him and to be honest, I don't want a relationship with anyone right now. He's asked a few times and told me I'm going to be his wife but the only man I'll ever marry is Abe.

I met him at my job a few weeks ago and as the manager, I had to train him. He was a fast learner but something told me this isn't where he wanted to be. Sure enough he confided in me, that this is just a job and he needed to stay out of jail. I was shocked my company hired him but then again he was in for drugs and this is an insurance company. No money is kept in the office so I guess they felt safe. Plus, my boss is black and he's all for giving back to the community. It is the first time he's done something like this though.

"Why you leave?"

"What you mean why I leave? You're standing there

basically fucking those chicks in front of me and we came together. I don't care what people think of me but damn, you could've showed a little more respect and took them outside or something." I told him and sat on the couch. I wasn't mad he was with those bitches but when Monica said something, it made me feel like shit. Who comes with someone and he's entertaining everyone but you?

"I know you're not mad." He had the nerve to say.

"Not at all Grady. I'm saying you could've handled that afterwards."

"I mean come on Honor, let's be real. You're not trying to fuck so I'm supposed to sit around and wait." He made his way to where I sat.

"Grady I'm sorry if you're under the impression I'm a quick ho. It's not who I am and I value what's between my legs. You may have tasted my sweetness but sliding in it, is something that takes me a long time to allow a man to do."

"Ok but its been a almost two months. How much longer do I have to wait?" He was kissing on my neck with his hands in my shorts and now my pussy was soaking wet. I'm sure after what he spoke of, he wants to fuck. I pushed his hand down further because it felt too good to make him stop.

"Let me take these off." I lifted up and his mouth connected with my clit in no time. My hand was on his head grinding all over his face. Once I came he didn't get up and made me have more and I wasn't complaining. He kissed up my stomach and I could hear him unzipping his jeans. This time I allowed him to continue. He was at my entrance and it felt like I came again.

"You ready ma?" He slid his tongue in my mouth and I nodded my head. He slipped in and I swear he felt so good but I stopped him.

"What's wrong?"

"Do you have a condom?"

"Shit Honor. I already been in it raw, please don't make me strap up."

"Grady we have to. Shitttt."

"See how good it feels." He put my legs on his shoulder.

"Damn Honor. You made me wait and I see why. You

about to have a nigga strung out."

"Grady shit you feel good too but you have to get up."
He picked me up and fucked me real good standing. I know we
should stop but I can't make him. I was lost in how he handled
me.

"You like that baby." I nodded my head yes and he sat
back on the couch. We had been sexing each other for at least
an hour but he had to stop twice because he was tired.

I began riding him and all of a sudden it dawned on me
that he was about to fuck two chicks at the party and if he
didn't wear a condom with me, he wasn't with them. Which
means he ran up in everyone raw.

"Why you stop?" He asked when I jumped off.

"You have to put one on or I'm done." He sucked his
teeth and started getting dressed.

"Are you serious?" I nodded my head yes.

"I'm not playing games with you Honor. You let me
fuck you this entire time and now you stop. This shit is over."

"Grady I don't want any kids and.-"

"Too late. I'm came in you twice already." He said and

slammed the door. Is that why he stopped those two times? *Oh hell no!* I threw some sweats on, grabbed my keys and ran out the door.

The whole way to the drug store all I could think of, is how he did it on purpose. This is the exact reason why I couldn't be with anyone now. Men played too many games and I refused to do it with them. I stormed in the store and walked down the aisle to get a plan b. Yup, a bitch ain't having no kids. I went to the register and ran into Monica. She saw what was in my hand and smirked.

"I guess you are fucking. You really should be more careful about who you let cum inside you." The cashier sucked her teeth.

"Mind your business." I put my item on the counter and paid the lady. I walked out the store and she was standing there grinning.

"Grady is fine as hell but honey he stays at the clinic. He's like Future when it comes to sex. He refuses to wear condoms. If I were you, I'd go to the clinic, I'm just saying. If you think Abe will want you after I tell him about this, you're mistaken. Toodles." The bitch said and I ran up on her and punched her in the face. I was over her talking shit. I grabbed her hair and slung her on the ground and started fucking her up even more.

"Let her go Honor." I heard someone say and looked up to see Noah.

"Fuck her. She always has something slick to say." I snatched my bag up off the ground and started walking to my car.

"I got something for you bitch."

"Yo, don't ever threaten her." I heard Noah say.

"Take your nasty ass home and clean that contaminated cum out your pussy." She said and sped off. Noah looked at me and I got in my car. Now I was embarrassed and hurt.

"I know you're not letting niggas run in you raw." He was holding my door open.

"It was a mistake and he told me when he left."

"Honor, you should know the difference. Did his dick get soft?" I shrugged my shoulders and told him what happened as far as him stopping. He said that's probably when he did it and he tried to get me pregnant on purpose. But why would he do that?

"Abe is going to blow his gasket when she tells him."

"Fuck that. He got her pregnant not too long ago."

"Honor, she was never pregnant by him. Abe, may be sleeping with her but that's one thing he'll never do with anyone but you." I stared at him and he was telling me the truth. Him and Noah are tight and he would've told him.

"I can't worry about him getting angry. He wasn't worried about me when I was laid up in the hospital because he was with her. Yea, I messed up but you see I'm making sure it goes no further than tonight. I'll see you later."

"What up?" He answered his phone and backed up. He gave me a look letting me know it was Abe. I pulled out and kept it moving.

****

"Bitchhhhhhhh what did you do?" Roxanne yelled in my ear bright and early this morning.

"What you mean?" I stretched my arms and yawned in the phone.

"Noah had to keep Abe from coming to your house, what was it, two weeks ago?"

"Really Roxanne, and you're just now calling me. He could've killed me by now."

"You haven't called me and I've been dealing with his mom and baby mama bullshit. Girl, Abe may wring your neck but he won't kill you. "

"Whatever." I started telling her the situation and she was ready to go fight Grady. Anyone could see he did the shit on purpose but lucky for me I took that pill and went crying in the Urgent Care clinic about my boyfriend being diagnosed with diseases. They gave me a shot of Penicillin and a Z pack to take for seven days. If he gave me anything. It was gone now.

I even had them do a rapid AIDS test. I'm going back to get the results of the blood one I took too and then I'm taking another one just in case. I had myself to blame for allowing it to get that far but he had no business taking it upon himself by releasing in me either.

"Why don't you stop the bullshit and get your man

back?"

"I want him Roxanne. I swear on everything he's all I think about and want but I'm not ready and neither is he."

"Why aren't you ready and you can't say, he's not because he's with her."

"I want him to love me with no distractions Roxanne. I don't want to walk in a club or a store and some chick can tell me she had him last night or the week before. I need him to want me like I want him. When he wakes up, I want to be all he thinks about. He's been in jail a long time and he needs time to get it all out of his system. When he does I'm going to get him back."

"Honor, it doesn't work like that. We all know he loves you but he's not going to sit around waiting forever. If you want Abe, its time you get over this fake ass fear you have and get him." I listened to what she said and decided today I would get him back. I hung the phone up and called, expecting him not to answer.

"Hello." I heard her voice and wanted to hang up but I'm not going to be petty.

"Can I speak to Abe?"

"Who the fuck is this?"

"Its Honor, Monica." She laughed.

"Baby, telephone." You could hear water running so I guess he was in the shower.

"Tell whoever it is, I'll call them back and get your ass in here and bend over." I heard him say and tears ran down my face.

"Welp! You heard him honey. I'm sorry but he wants his pussy first. I think its more important than any bullshit you're calling for. Don't call him again." She hung up in my ear.

I dropped my phone and got dressed for the day. I called Chelsea on her cell and asked if she wanted to hang out with me and we could pick Precious up. She told me she'd be ready and that she's at her grandma's. I drove over there, she hopped in the car and we went to Roxanne's where Precious was outside waiting. The two of them had me take them to the mall, out to eat and then we went back to Roxanne's house. We all got out and walked in. Noah, Abe and a few other guys were in the living room playing a game.

I spoke to Noah and the other guys and went in the kitchen to see what Roxanne was doing. This nut had a bridal magazine out on the table open. I checked her fingers to see if she was engaged and she said the magazine is out to give him a hint. She was crazy and I remember Abe telling me he would ask her soon. I picked lil man up and fed his chunky ass. She made Junior and Melody come down and get some of the pizza and wings the guys ordered.

We both grabbed some food and sat down talking. We had gone through a bottle of wine and were on the second one. I was a little tipsy and the more drank, I felt it stronger. I hugged her and said I would see her tomorrow. I had to get over here more often.

By the time I got home, it was after ten and all I wanted to do was go to sleep but I had to shower the day off. We ran around so much, my body was sweating and I couldn't sleep like that. I had to hold on to the shower walls to keep from falling. I guess when you don't drink a lot; the little you taste will have you feeling real nice. I turned off the water, dried off and got in my bed naked. I fell asleep as soon as my head hit the pillow.

I woke up to use the bathroom but I refused to get out the bed. Someone was in my house and I heard them coming up the steps. I hid under my covers thinking they'll think I'm sleep and go away. It was pitch dark in my room so I couldn't see even if I tried to peek.

I laid there holding my breath in and praying the person wouldn't kill me. The bed had a dip in it at the edge and I started crying because I didn't want to be raped again. I could hear them removing their jeans because of the buckle and prayed to God he was watching over me.

I gripped the blankets tighter when the person tried to remove them. I started screaming, kicking and trying to scoot off the bed. The person held my arms down and climbed on top of me. I kept screaming please stop but he kissed my neck and moved up to my mouth. I turned my face and he took one of his hands and stopped me from moving.

"If you ever give my pussy away again, I'll kill you and I mean it." Abe said and moved off me. I smacked him and he laughed like it was funny. I ran out the room to use the bathroom because I definitely went on myself. I grabbed a washcloth and cleaned my pussy up.

"Why are you here Abe?" I asked staring at him flipped through the channels. I'm not even going to ask how he got my address. Roxanne and Noah wanted us back together so bad, I'm sure they handed it to him with no problem but how the hell did he get in?

"I'm here for you Honor. I know it was you on the phone earlier."

"Then why did you let her speak to me like that?"

"I didn't know at first but when she got in the shower smirking, I knew then. I hopped out and left her in their alone. Baby, I'm not into those childish as games she's doing."

"Abe, I called to tell you.-"

"You don't have to. I already know you want me."

"How?"

"You haven't called me in weeks, maybe even months and you hit me up. I figured you were ready and left her."

"Now what?"

"Now you're my woman and don't worry about Grady. That shit is going to get handled."

"Abe, I don't want you back in jail." I climbed on top of him and he shut the television off. His fingertips were combing my back and landed on my ass.

"How did you get in here?"

"Roxanne gave me her key and I made a copy." I smacked him on the arm. Roxanne is the only one who had a key to my place and now him. She hated that I lived alone and said she needed one in case I went missing.

"Do you like when I have sex with you?" I know he asked because I up and left him alone.

"Yesssss." I moaned when he flipped me over and dipped two fingers inside me.

"Are you sure?" He didn't give me anytime to answer and forced his way inside.

"Got dammit your shit is tight. I'm sorry Honor but I'm about to cum." He said after only being on top after a few minutes.

"Then let me swallow it." He stopped stroking and

wrapped his hand around my throat.

"You sucked that niggas dick?" I scratched his arms and he let go.

"No Abe. Get off me." I punched him in the chest and he moved.

"I'm sorry Honor. Its bad enough you were reckless with the other shit."

"Abe, if you ever lay your hands on me again, I will never speak to you again."

"I'm sorry." He pulled me on top and we began kissing again. I kissed and sucked down his body and let him instruct me on what to do. It took me a few minutes to get use to having something this big in my mouth. He told me what to do with my tongue, how to jerk him at the same time I sucked his balls and how to hum.

The shit turned me on hearing him moan and grab my hair. He told me to get up because I wasn't ready for big girl things but I proved him wrong and had him gripping the sheets; saying my name as I swallowed his seeds. He laid there breathing fast for a few minutes.

"Sit on my face." I did what he said and rode his tongue and mouth until my legs gave out.

"Lets try this again." He said and entered me.

"I love you Abe and I'm sorry for making you wait and taking you through the bullshit. Yessss baby, right there. Oh yea." My body started shaking again and this time he lifted my legs and pushed them behind my ears. He dug so deep, I literally screamed out.

"Yea baby. I love hitting this spot." He hit something deep in me that had my eyes rolling every time.

"Have my baby Honor."

"Abe."

"There's no Abe. Yes is all I want to hear." He hit that spot again and it felt as if water was gushing out my pussy. I've never come as hard and strong as I just did.

"Damn Honor, you wet as fuck. Shittttt." He pounded faster and soon after laid on top of me.

"You just got pregnant and if you even think about taking your ass down to the store, I'm fucking you up."

"I'm not baby. If it's meant to be, it will happen." He

kissed me and his dick was hard again. He had me all over the room and bed all night and a bitch didn't complain. Abe had a great sex game and I never should've let that bitch have him. You can believe she won't anymore. His phone started ringing and it was de ja vu. Monica was calling and he was in the shower. I'm not going to answer but I am taking the phone to him.

"What?" He answered in the phone and made me get in with him.

"I told you it was over when she was ready." I heard him say as I ran a rag down his body with soap. His dick jumped at my touch and he smiled.

"Get him right so I can make love to you." I kissed his neck and stroked him with my hands. He grew with each touch and I jumped in his arms.

"Oh shit Abe." I moaned out, ignoring him on the phone. I could hear her yelling about him not being shit and why did he leave her. I couldn't focus anymore because Abe was hitting my spot.

"Monica, I gotta go. My girl's about to cum all over my

dick and I need to enjoy it. Shit, Honor. You look so fucking beautiful right now." The phone dropped and he gave me the best dick lashing ever again. You could hear Monica screaming but neither of us stopped. Eventually she'll hang up and if she doesn't oh well.

Abe

A nigga happy as hell Honor made the decision to be with me. I'm not even going to front, over the last month since we've made it official, it's been nothing but love. I wake up and she's either giving me head or making me breakfast. At night, we'd have sex or watch movies until we fell asleep.

Chelsea has basically been staying here with us too. Once she found out, her ass packed some clothes and begged Honor to stay at my house with us. Hell yea, she moved in. It took her a few days but she gave in. Noah and I had a few people come help us move her stuff. There's no going back to an apartment. If she gets mad, there are more than enough rooms in the house to sulk in.

This morning I was making my way to Monica's to let her know this calling me all hours of the night and sending me screen shots of her naked has to stop. It's crazy how she didn't want me cheating on her but has no problem trying to get me to do it to Honor.

I parked in front of her house and sent my girl a text saying I love you. I'm not about to do anything but she wasn't too keen on me coming here. I try to keep her in the loop so we don't have any secrets.

"I missed you baby." She reached out to hug me and I put the phone in my pocket. I made sure to leave it on record. Monica would surely say it was more than it was.

"Back up. I came to ask you not to send me those messages and pictures. My girl doesn't appreciate that shit."

"Fuck her." She shut the door and I went upside her head like a kid. I was raised not to hit women but I'll pop the fuck out of her. It was an accident when I choked Honor. The thought of her giving a man any pleasure bothered me.

"Now all of a sudden you're worried about her." She walked around in some small ass shorts and I noticed her stomach is bigger than normal.

"It's always been about her but what I'm trying to figure out is, how you got pregnant." She pulled the shirt down further but it was too late.

"I wasn't going to tell you since you're all up in her ass."

"Try again shorty. I know for a fact that isn't my baby.

I've never slept with you raw and I always pull out before I nut. Whoever you were sleeping with may want to be made aware." I stood up to leave.

"Fuck you Abe. This is your.-" she was about to speak until she saw the look on my face.

"If you call, text or send any shit to my phone, I'm sending someone over here to fuck you up. Matter of fact, I'm sure Honor wouldn't mind digging in your ass again." I smirked and opened the door to leave. I turned around and she stood there with her face turned up. Oh well, she better find the nigga she pregnant by and see if he wants her.

****

I drove over to Vera's house next to put her ass in check. As usual, there were mad niggas outside but they all gave me respect when I walked up. One of the guys came over and told me to watch Vera because she was telling someone Honor is going to get what's coming to her. I nodded my head and thanked him for telling me. That's the good thing about being cool with everyone. They still had your back regardless if you were in the game or not.

I stepped in the house and it appeared to be a little clean but not enough where my daughter would be here. She's not trying to leave from around Honor anyway. Precious is even over all the time now and the two of them are a mess together. This house is a straight hang out spot.

I heard loud music upstairs and followed the sound. I opened the door and was shocked, however, expected it from a nigga like him. Ernest was fucking some chick on the floor who seemed as if she weren't into it. His back was turned so he didn't see me standing there. I went to shut the door but noticed the chick crying and mouthing the words "*help me*".

I wasn't sure what to do because if she wasn't enjoying it, she should tell him. But then again, this nigga is a rapist and if that's what he's doing, I should help. I turned the music off and he stopped to see what was going on. The girl tried to scoot from under him but he laid on top and asked why did I turn it off.

"Get up." He laughed like it was funny.

"Man go head. This my girl and how you walking in while we fucking?"

"This your man shorty?"

"No. Please help.-" he punched her so hard in the face she passed out.

"Yo, what the fuck wrong with you?" I pushed him off her and covered her up with a sheet. I was getting ready to lift her up when his stupid ass swung on me. I started fucking him up so bad he tried to grab the broom to hit me with it. I clipped him and had his ass on the ground. I started stomping and kicking him.

"Abe please stop." I heard Vera in my ear but it didn't matter. This motherfucker had me fucked up. It took a few dudes to get me off.

"What did you do?" Vera ran over to him. I snatched her up by the back of her head.

"You allowing this nigga to rape chicks in your house? What the fuck wrong with you?"

"He didn't rape her. She came up here willingly."

"Does that look like a female who came up here willingly?" I pointed to the girl knocked out on the floor.

"Ask your girl. She did the same thing." My head

snapped and she had a smirk on her face.

"You saying he raped Honor?" I walked up on her and she backed away until she hit the wall.

"I'm saying she was up here in the bathroom.-" I started squeezing the life out of her.

"The video you sent me was him, wasn't it?" Her eyes were bulging.

"You knew he did that and not only did you keep it a secret, but my daughter has been here with him too." I squeezed tighter and her face was turning blue.

"Abe, come on man." The guy struggled but was able to remove my hands from her throat. Her eyes were rolling in her head. I kneeled down to her ear.

"You thought I would run to you if I saw that. You're a stupid bitch and because of it, my daughter won't ever step foot in this house again." I nudge the chick a little to wake her up.

"Please get me out of here." I nodded my head at the dude and he took her downstairs.

"This is for all the bullshit you and him caused." I took my gun out and let two off in his head. I'm not sure she saw what happened because my gun had a silencer on it and she was still gasping for air.

"If you even think about going to the cops I will come back." I kicked her one good time in the face and left out the room.

"Someone is on the way. Get these motherfuckers out of here." I went to my car and called Honor. I asked her to meet me at the hospital. I had to calm her down and say I was ok because she thought something happened to me.

"I've been watching you and I like how you roll. Hit me up later so we can talk." I told Charlie, who is the dude that told me what Vera said and was now making everyone leave. I got a text from my peoples saying they'd be there to clean up in two minutes. I took shorty to the hospital, walked in with her in my arms and told them she was raped and I found her like that.

"Thank you." She said when they placed her on a stretcher.

"Anytime. You need me to call someone."

"No. When you were talking to the guys, I called my

dad. He's on the way."

"I'll wait for someone to show up. As far as dude, you never have to worry about him again." She gave me a big hug and out the corner of my eye I saw Honor, Roxanne and Noah. My mom came in and so did Noah's. I saw the way my aunt stared at Roxanne, but she ain't crazy enough to talk shit in front of Noah.

"What's going on?" Honor looked like she was about to cry. She probably thought I was cheating on her or that I did.

"I'll see you later." I told the girl and went to Honor.

"Why didn't you tell me?"

"Tell you what?" I grabbed her hand and moved away from everyone.

"Vera's brother. Did he do that shit to you? Is that him on the video?"

"Who told you?"

"I went to see her and Honor he was doing the same thing to her. Vera came in after I beat his ass for swinging on me and mentioned it." She covered her mouth.

"Oh my God. I have to speak to the doctors."

"What? Why?"

"Abe, the day you saw me and my face was messed up it's because he gave me oral herpes." I frowned my face up.

"I have to tell them so they can treat her." She ran over and asked for the doctor. I let my family know I was fine and they could go. Honor had called them after I called her, saying I had to come here. She didn't believe I was ok.

"What's going on?" Noah said to Jose. He was the connect we had been speaking to and having meetings with lately. He wanted us to get back in the game but we declined.

"Hey you two. I came up to see someone." He's always been secretive about shit but he looked nervous as hell. Jose was about forty-two maybe and still had his young appearance.

"I'm ready to go." Honor said and I told Jose we would catch him later. The chick won't know I left and could probably care less. As long as she was away from the rapist, she's good. After we got home, Honor sat on the couch while I went to take a shower.

"I didn't know how to tell you." She said stepping in

with me. I lifted her face.

"Never be afraid to tell me anything. You never have to worry about seeing him again." I smiled.

"I'm pregnant."

"Say word."

"Word. I found out today. Three weeks, to be exact."

"Damn baby, you just made me the happiest man out here." I stopped and stared at her.

"He checked and no the baby's not in my tubes this time."

"Thank you Honor for coming back and giving me what no other woman can." We ended up sexing each other all night. I was living the life and no one could tell me different.

"He knows about the baby." Monica said in the phone as Kasha was giving me head. Her pussy may be trash but the head is decent. I hadn't seen her in a few weeks so when she hit me up; I let her come break me off.

"How?" I asked getting ready to nut. I had to bite down on my lip to keep the moan threatening to escape. Monica was aware of Kasha but she didn't know I still dealt with her on a sexual level.

"My stomach has a slight pouch in it." I heard her but couldn't answer because my voice was caught as Kasha took her time sucking and taking my seeds out. I disconnected the call without another word and tossed the phone.

"Shitttttt. Got damn girl." I lifted her head up and she had a grin on her face.

"Feels good huh?" She stripped and my dick sprang to life again. Yea the pussy ain't good or let's say what I'm used to, but if my man can wake up at the sight of her being naked, then I'm going in. I snatched a condom off the dresser, rolled it down and plunged my way inside.

"Right there Duke. Oh yea baby." She started throwing it back and I had to stop and look at her. Not only was the pussy super wet, but feeling good. I yanked her hair and fucked her harder. Shorty kept up with me and even had me sit while she rode the hell out of me. I heard my phone going off but ignored it because this pussy here had me gone for the moment.

"What's different?" I asked when we finished and were getting dressed.

"What you mean?"

"Your pussy has never been that good or wet. Have you been fucking someone else and they showed you?" I saw her roll her eyes. I didn't mean to sound harsh but I'm not into telling woman what they want to hear. She walked in front of me and wrapped her arms around my waist.

"Duke you are the only man I'm sleeping with."

"Ok so what's the change?" I put my sneakers on and looked down at my phone. Monica had called me fifteen times. Kasha whispered something but I couldn't hear. I asked her to repeat herself.

"I stopped getting high." I looked up from my phone and that's when I noticed her body had changed. I didn't pay it any mind when we were fucking but now I see it. She no longer had bags under her eyes and gained a few pounds. Kasha wasn't a fiend or anything like that but she definitely got high just about everyday.

"Oh yea."

"Yea. After the party we were at, I noticed you were disgusted with me. Once you dropped me off, I went to the hospital and they sent me straight to a rehab. I thought about fighting it but if you were going to take me serious, it had to be when I was sober."

"Kasha, you know.-"

She quieted my mouth with hers and for the first time, I gave into it. She had been trying to kiss me since the first time we hooked up. I always declined because everyone knows kissing brings emotions.

"Mmmmmm damn Kasha." I said when we separated.

"I know you're with her but I'm hoping you'll realize,

she isn't who you think." She grabbed her things and left.

I picked my phone up and scrolled through the missed calls and texts. I couldn't help but think about what Kasha said as far as Monica not being who she claims. As far as I know, she has never tried any sneaky shit with me but then again, she's the one who had those women drug Noah, and to this day she won't tell me why. It's not as if she were sleeping with him.

I called Monica back and all she did was bitch and complain about Abe going back to the Honor chick. I don't understand why the hell she's up in arms over it, when she's been fucking me. Never mind the fact, Abe doesn't tell her anything, so the entire fake relationship thing didn't work out. I hung up on her because not once did she give me anything to use against him.

I thought back to what Kasha said and decided to have someone watch Monica. If she's up to something, I want to know what it is. If she'll turn against Abe who I can tell she has feelings for, then she'll definitely turn against me. I called Grady and told him we needed to speak ASAP. A storm is brewing and if Kasha's right, Monica is the one bringing it to life.

I felt bad for the woman Vera's brother raped. Honestly, I'm glad Abe was there to save her because it's obvious no one else was. I couldn't wait to see Vera again. Abe told me she seemed to be happy her brother did that nasty shit to me. If you ask me, I'd say she is as sick as him and the entire family should disappear, except for Chelsea.

Now that little girl had my heart from the first day I met her. She was definitely spoiled but Abe made sure to get in her ass when needed. He always told her, he'd do anything for her but the minute she got out of line he would let her know.

A few times she ran to me to save her but I never did. Not because I didn't want to but because I would never step in while he disciplined her nor would I overturn a punishment. The minute that happens, her ass will be worse than she is.

I was on my way to the store when I noticed two black SUV's behind me. When I turned so did they. I wasn't scared but I did call Abe and let him know. He asked where I was and told me to drive to the address he gave me. I did and when I got there Noah and a bunch of other dudes were outside.

The trucks pulled up behind me and I saw nothing but guns drawn. I hit the floor fast as hell and waited for the gunfire to end. After a few minutes of hearing nothing, my door opened and I pointed my gun at the person. Abe never let me leave home without it.

"Calm down sis." Noah said pushing my hand away. He helped me get out my car and pointed to where Abe was.

"Who is that? Are those the guys who followed me?" I saw a Spanish looking dude and some other guys who could be his security standing there. The closer I got, the more familiar the guys face became. It was the same one who showed up at the hospital when Abe found the girl.

"Honor meet Jose. Jose this is my soon to be wife, Honor." He lifted my hand and kissed the back of it.

"You doing too much Jose." Abe smacked his hand down and they started laughing.

"I wanted to thank you personally for informing the doctors about the guy who violated my daughter." I stared at him in a confused way.

211

"I'm sorry. I don't know who you're speaking of." *Was his daughter the one Ernest raped?*

"The woman Abe brought to the hospital is my daughter." I looked him up and down. He couldn't have been any older than thirty and the chick looked to be twenty.

"Honor don't get fucked up staring that hard."

"Whatever. Anyway, how is she?"

"She's better. Unfortunately, she contracted the disease." I could see his anger building.

"If he wasn't dead, I swear I'd torture the fuck out of him."

"I'm sorry to hear that." I told him and put my head down.

"I wish I mentioned it sooner to someone because maybe it wouldn't have happened to her." Abe pulled me in his arms and hugged me.

"Never think like that Honor. It was more women before you who never spoke a word either. He should've never been released from jail." Jose said and handed me an envelope. I opened it up, looked in it, then

212

up at him and handed it back.

"Don't insult me." He pushed it back.

"I can't accept this."

"It's for you because your man won't take it and he saved her. You didn't have to reveal your secret to make sure my daughter got the best care. I will forever be in debt to both of you."

"I'm happy we could help and this isn't necessary."

"Please take it. My daughter would have a fit if she found out you refused her money."

"Take it Honor." Abe whispered in my ear. It wasn't a sexy one, but more of a, do it or else.

"Fine." I took it and put it in my pocket.

"What's your daughters name?"

"Ciara."

"Ok well, with this money I'm going to open a safe haven for women who are the victim of rape and any other abuse and name it after her. It's the least I can do since you won't take it back. And she has to be my partner on it or I promise to rip this check up." He chuckled and looked at Abe.

"You got a live one on your hands."

"I know and I love it."

"I'll see you later and I'll make sure Ciara gets in contact with you. She may not want to come here but she will call." I nodded my head and watched him walk away.

"Baby this is too much money for mentioning a disease." I stared at the check for thirty million dollars.

"He's happy his daughter was saved. Yes, she suffered a rape but what if he killed her? Or if they didn't find out about the disease until it was too late and she couldn't have kids. He's not the type to go around handing out money or even thanking people for helping. He's the type who feels like it's owed to him, so to have two complete strangers save his daughter, it means a lot. Well I'm not a stranger but I didn't know she was his daughter." I smiled and stared at him.

"Don't start that shit out here." Noah said and walked away shaking his head.

"What? We didn't even do anything." Abe started laughing.

"You don't have to baby. He knows what's about to happen."

"Oh yea. What's that?" I asked walking to my truck.

"This." He helped me in the truck and turned me to face him. He stood in front of me and stuck his right hand in my pants. I had to kiss him to suppress the moan leaving my lips.

"Let it go Honor." He said and went back to kissing me. My bottom half grinded on his fingers until I couldn't hold out any longer. I stopped kissing him and literally sucked the hell out of his neck. By the time I calmed down he had a huge hickey.

"Can I slide up in you real quick?" I saw someone walking towards us out the corner of my eye.

"So this what you do out in public?" Abe moved his hand and sucked on his fingers in front of her.

"Yup. The pussy taste real good too." I watched him walk up to Monica.

"I don't know why you're here or how you knew we were but it's in your best interest to leave."

"Why Abe? You don't want her to know the last time you came over we had sex." I jumped out the truck and he had to hold me back. I saw Noah and a few other dudes coming our way.

"I heard everything that went down and honey if I were you, I'd find my baby daddy because this one right here is mine.

We'll be raising our little one without your fake ass pregnancy."

"You're pregnant?"

"Yup and if you even think.-" I didn't finish because she swung over Abe and punched me in the face. I tried to hit her but Noah stopped me.

"Let her go Abe." Noah said holding me. Abe had Monica against the wall with a gun under her chin and the other hand was wrapped around her throat.

"Nah Noah. She thinks this is a game." I snatched away from Noah when a gunshot went off. I thought Abe shot her but it was Duke coming in our direction. *What the hell is going on?*

I was glad to see Duke coming towards me. I saw the look in Abe's eyes and he for sure was about to kill me. Everyone told me how he was when it came to Honor but to see it with my own eyes is another thing. It made what I was about to do, worth it. I hated this bitch and she's about to pay for the hurt and pain she caused my family.

Abe removed the gun from my chin but his grip on my throat hadn't weakened and I was still struggling to get away. I continued smacking his hand. Once he noticed Honor speaking to Duke, he forgot about me and made his way to them. I found my way to a spot and hid there so no one would see me.

I made sure to remain hidden so I wouldn't get hit with a stray. A few minutes later I heard Abe telling Honor to leave and he'll be home shortly. She did a bunch of crying and saying she didn't want to leave him. I heard them kissing and my anger grew. The door shut and she pulled off. It didn't take long for more gunshots to go off.

"Talk that shit now bitch." I said jumping out the backseat and into the front. She stopped the car and I punched her in the face again. I began stabbing her anywhere I could. I'm no killer so I felt crazy sticking this hunters knife in her body. Who knew it would puncture her skin and go so deep? I saw terror in her eyes as well as her tears.

"This is for my brother and cousin bitch." I said. I opened the door and kicked her the fuck out. I jumped out and started stomping her in the stomach over and over. Abe didn't deserve anymore kids. I drove over to my next destination and parked.

"Roxanne, you need to get over to second street. Honor is bleeding and I think she's dying." I yelled in the phone and hung up. Just like I thought, she came running out the house and hopped in her car. I followed her and once she stopped at the light, I ran this truck into the back and didn't stop until it hit a big ass pole. The shit cracked in half and fell on top of her car.

Mission Accomplished!

To Be Continued...

Made in United States
Orlando, FL
13 August 2022